"The number of hypotheses available to explain any given phenomenon is infinite, Robert M.Pirsig."

PRESUMED LOST

A novel by
David Dow Millar

There are winners and losers in life. It is unfair but nature is not sentimental while God never promised heaven on earth.

Everyone has known friends who have gone off the radar, disappeared, and never heard off again. Did they reach their promised land or did fate divert them? Being in the wrong place at the wrong time is a throw of the dice unforeseeable by Man. Old friends are forgotten, presumed lost.

A remindful depiction of how the fabric that holds society together can rapidly fall away allowing primeval forces to surface.

4

First published in Great Britain in 2016

Copyright @ David Dow Millar 2016

First Published 2016 by The Misty Tree

The moral right of the author has been asserted

All rights reserved.

ISBN 978-0-9929340-6-4

Ebook ISBN 978-0-9929340-7-1

DISCLAIMER

All characters and places mentioned in this novel are fictitious and any inference to real people, dead or alive, is coincidental. Any familiarity is simply because most people's lives, events, hopes and dreams are similar, and the interpretation is only different.

This is a tale about how breaking the bonds that tie people together leads to isolation. Past actions leave imprints and affect future events, and exerting too much effort on fulfilling a dream can be detrimental to necessary bridge building that securely anchors you.

The moment you discover true values, it is too late. In the end, it is only the final understanding of them that is fulfilling.

CONTENTS

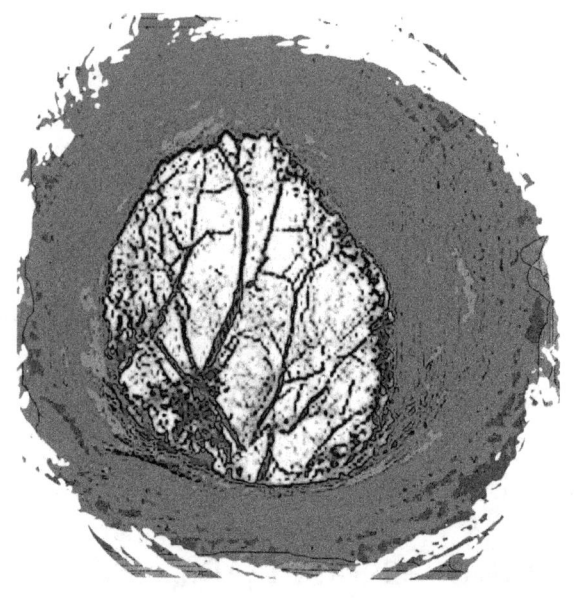

"Whoever digs a pit will fall into it, and he who rolls a stone will have it roll back on him, Proverbs 26:27, King James Bible."

PAYS DE LAMARTINE

The profit makers had opened up the world by
making travel affordable, easy and quick, enriching
life for anyone with an up and go attitude.
Nonetheless, for this childless husband and wife in
their late-fifties near neighbours France remained
their favourite destination.

It was great to get away from it all when the schools
were back, leaving behind overcast streets with
shoulders crouched to minimise the effect of hard
rain brought in by cold autumnal winds. Their mode
of transport was a four-wheeled drive silver *Renault
Safrane*, designed for comfort, to catch some late sun
in *le Midi*. The colours to be found in a late
September break made all the packing and tedious
hotel arrangements worthwhile for these
Francophiles; including hours spent sitting in travel
agents going over the itinerary to make sure rooms
were booked on the correct dates of arrival.

The contented pair had been living the good life for several years now, ever since both took early retirement from white-collar jobs when a generous inheritance came their way. The man had worked for a large private company with a monopoly on a sought-after product and the woman was a teacher who reached the heights of deputy head at a primary school. The grand plan was to retire at the start of the new millennium but a death in the family accelerated these plans for a relaxed post-work existence. Both were northerners concerned about social justice but not so daft as not to accept the benefits offered by a right-wing government. One was a self-deluded infallible character, infinitely ready to pounce on anyone that was not in accordance with his view. He believed whatever came out of his mouth was true because he said it. Having seen the green reflected light of the aurora borealis, it became an indisputable fact that the aurora was only ever that colour, not red, blue or purple, just green. The other wanted a settled ordered life, so avoided any domestic kerfuffle. This was achieved by always remembering to agree with her husband. She had learnt to show immense patience and obedience. Years of being a public servant taught her to be good at portraying willingness to follow orders. However, there was a great difference between feelings and showing.

The pair loved to proclaim to all and sundry how adorable it was to dawdle through the Gallic countryside admiring its undulating beauty. Good early-received pensions easily helped them pay for the petrol consumed by the ever-hungry guzzler.

Joined at the hip, she was the navigator and road watcher as her partner drove. The poems of *La Fontaine* on her lap, resting on the spread-out roadmap. As the car made its way, glimpses and half-remembered impressions of the country flicked through their eyes. Their generation had it all with afternoon TV bomb blasted with emotive adverts from companies wanting their money: second homes, expensive furniture, luxury kitchens, holidays and investments for them and their grandchildren. No advert ever mentioned taking responsibility for surviving octogenarian parents or ageing relatives. Nor did it bother the couple that theirs was the generation that had a relatively easy road to follow resulting in consequent generations having to pick up the bill for the unforeseen additional state and pension provisions required to maintain higher than expected numbers in a long old age. There again, why should this couple have any qualms, after all, they had no children. The man believed he deserved what he got and the wife was that type of woman who was forever surprised by how little, compared to her, her mother could live on.

The further the distance from home, the more romance travel created, solidifying the illusion of beauty in everything seen into an idyllic way of life far away from the urban rat race. Driving along, a multitude of small partitioned fields separated by wooden fencing, rusty barbed wire, and hedges or dry-stone walls, many in disrepair, inundated the eyes. All signalled the presence of small hold farms owned by the same generations of contented families. The journey gave them a sense of surreal magic, full of joy fuelled by unexpected stunning and strange sights. The litter of broken bottles, rusty tins, old prams or discarded farm machinery conveniently ignored or hidden by long grass in summer and morning ground mist in autumn.

They were fans of the claret and burgundy. The year before, after leaving the *Dover* to *Calais* ferry the car headed down to *Bordeaux* through the *Dordogne* to allow them to savour the delights of its Atlantic influenced wines and cheeses, before cutting inland to the rose city of *Toulouse* on to the medieval fortress town of *Carcassonne* leading to *le Midi*. This autumn, a different route to '*le paradis*' had been planned. The vineyards of *Côte d'Or, Saône-et-Loire* and *Rhône* would have the pleasure of their visits. After all, burgundy was an autumnal colour. Days spent touring fields that have been used for viniculture for centuries with nights in picturesque towns waiting to be roamed. These regions were full of Chateaux, Abbeys, richly decorated churches and a multitude of rivers to feed the thirsty grapes. From these regions, Abbots sent Benedictine and Cistercian monks to save Europe and in return, gathered rents filled the coffers of *Cluny* and *Fontenay*. Powerful secular residents also sent missionaries: the armies of the Dukes of Burgundy occupied neighbouring territories and demanded tribute. The gold had flooded in, allowing these long-gone rulers to be still remembered.

The first part of the journey used the motorways to get to as soon as possible the chosen regions to explore. Thereafter only local roads would be considered. The plan to find their favourite vineyards got off to a good start. In northern Burgundy, after a small disagreement over her navigation skills the road through the well-known dry white wine vineyards of *Chablis* was found. The sight of vines on rolling hills with patches of green, red and golden brown amongst a sea of yellow confronted them.

From there, an overnight stay in *Dijon* to commence *la route de Grand Cru* in the morning. They found busy *Dijon* a confusing place to negotiate but once in the *centre de ville,* an ancient university town revealed itself, a town that once was the effective medieval centre of France and like the Atlantic coast dukedoms were allied with the Plantagenet Kings to keep this country partitioned. To their delight, a discovered Indian restaurant provided some home fare. The couple were accordingly put in the best of spirits. In many ways, the red wine of Burgundy suited their palate, as earthy red went with most food the traditional meat and two veg carnivores ate, especially on a Sunday. Sunday lunch was tasteless without a couple of bottles of red. Coming from the North the weather imposed a diet of stodge made up of hotpots, stews, roasts and pies. Holidays in the *le Midi* gave them the opportunity to appreciate a lighter *repas*. Soft leaf salads full of contrasting flavours, different types of cured meats and just caught that morning Mediterranean fish served with flamed cooked vegetables demanded a crisp refreshment to accompany them. Sitting outside, every meal became an occasion to enjoy and spending a late afternoon downing a few bottles of white Burgundy made more sense in a warmer climate.

In the morning, the drive through limestone landscapes that allowed *grand cru* wines to be created enthralled them. First stop was at the vineyards of *Chambolle-Musigny*. Some bottles made from the pinot grape were safely deposited in the boot of the car after a tour and tasting. Next, lunch was sought in the town of *Nuits-Saint-Georges*. After a leisurely walk along its tight high streets, peering into an array of shops selling wine, what else, to the tourist trade, the couple headed for the next vineyard tour, this time to sample a chardonnay grape wine. A rarity found in a golden triangle surrounded by the red grape. Accordingly, some bottles of *Le Clos Blanc de Vougeot* from the vineyard in *Savigny-lès-Beaune* were placed next to the already bought appetising wines to be drunk once the holiday home was reached. The planned stayover that night was *Beaune*, a town built by merchants to house wines in cellars down its quiet streets. The wealth and importance of the town since medieval times reflected in the richness of its hospices to help the church feed the needy and aid entry into the afterlife for its benefactors.

The following day, they leisurely circled round the vineyards of *Santenay,* enjoying the more robust and cheaper pinot wines of this area. The night was spent in *Chalon-sur-Saône*, one of many similar sized towns that owed its existence to the wide flowing waters. A distribution point for wines to travel along the river and canal arteries of the country. Time proven transport systems still heavy used by a country that refused to be rushed. Here a chill box was filled with the cheeses of the region: *Chaource* to go with the Burgundian whites, *Epoisses* for the reds, and *Soumaintrain* with the Chablis. So, ended a scrumptious stay in *Côte d'Or,* the next part of the tour was the vineyards of *Saône-et-Loire.*

The next day, the holidaymakers deliberately got up early, skipped breakfast and headed on the road so that good time was made with a late morning brunch further south as a reward. Unfortunately, just ten minutes out of town they went right instead of straight on when a temporary diversion mislead both the navigator and the driver. The instructions had flashed past too quickly for them to understand. The couple drove unaware of the easily made error, as the road looked as if to be heading in the correct direction. However, there would not be an approaching junction to lead them onto the better-maintained signposted routes into *Saône-et-Loire.* Doubts started to cross the mind of the navigator when she did not see the *Saône* or signs suggesting it would shortly appear on the left.

"Everything will be all right," hoped the navigator. She was easily flustered when quick decisions had to be made and accordingly tried to put them off until the last moment.

"All part of the adventure, see the real France," she reassuringly said to the driver while trying to appear phlegmatic.

Like a bumpy car journey, their relationship dallied along where one narcissistically exploited the empathy of the other. However, even when everything looked tranquil, there was always an undercurrent present due to past misdemeanours, grievances and intimate knowledge of each other's habits; a list of many little things that could quickly stop them treating each other with respect. Seldom did the driver voice appreciation of the virtues of the navigator. She hated his peevish criticism of her map reading and his continual freely enunciated concern about the low level of the fuel gauge indicator.

Uncertainty worked its way into both minds, as any passed road sign only indicated the names of houses, artisan workshops and farms. There was nothing of any substantial size to pinpoint the car's location on the map. They had veered off the tourist track onto back roads that the locals knew without the need for easily understood road signs. The world of vineyards and happy smiling patrons with wares to sell had been left behind. The tourist route signposts every five hundred metres were not just beacons to the next place of interest but markers to ensure the holidaymaker stayed on a safe path, not to roam off and get lost, to become trapped in inescapable labyrinths.

On one road the couple came upon a ruined mill, a roofless corpse with sprawling walls and timbers, behind it could be glimpsed rusting vehicles, it conjured up an image of urban decay in the middle of the countryside. Down another road, they spotted a farmer standing in the middle of his crops, wreathed in a mist, peeing to his heart's content. The shaft of his scythe was rammed into the soil next to him, with low light glinting off the blade. The female was transfixed and projected her own feelings onto the possible designs of this man towards her if she was found alone with him.

"It's the length of a water hose," gasped the female.

"What is it?"

"Nothing, dear."

An indignant expression flashed across the face of the driver.

The sight of the long penis reminded the female passenger of the time in her youth at college when she and some other girls allowed a *Don Juan* to have his way with them. A layabout who she fondly remembers as being cute and who had completely forgotten that night with flirty girls that delivered the goods. He was only taken advantage of silly girls wanting to be flower children.

The thought of her wild college days, made her visibly blush and shudder. After college when real life kicked in, a dread overwhelmed her, and for many years filled her with melancholic thoughts about the future, which firmly persuaded her to settle for mister grumpy when that opportunity came along in her early thirties.

The terrain had changed. Far from the tourist spots,

the atmosphere took on a macabre character. Down in the valleys, away from limestone cliffs, the woods were thicker and the exposed land pitted and rugged. The car radio prattled on and off with only a few words or phrases carrying any meaning to these tourists. A fine misty drizzle cut visibility down to a few hundred yards on an almost colourless early morning tinted in a slight blue haze. In the gloom of this light, the mist rolled, as in a dream, along the valley floor, swallowing up the livestock in the far edges of fields. The rustic houses were dead to the world in this remote setting, haunting almost with any structural defects or decay blurred by the dullness. Only if the car were on higher ground would they see clear enough into the distance.

As the car continued running down the fuel gauge, the roads became tree covered single lanes that weaved and swerved round natural outcrops and streams. Several times the road turned into a dirt track then disappeared altogether and presented them with an unpassable dead end: a locked gate or a saturated field that was no better than a mud bank that only a local expert knew how to cross. These dead-ends ate up time and petrol by forcing them to reverse and revisit the last junction crossed to take a punt at a different route. The confused travellers glimpsed what looked like a desired arterial road only to not be able to find a way to it. Driving in tight unmarked right-hand roads in a right hand steered car did not help the driver's blood pressure. What made matters worse the tank was not filled the night before when they had the chance. The driver insisted enough was in the tank to get them to the next destination. So now, instead of avoiding location names that meant nothing to them, the holidaymakers commenced to drive up and down hollows in the hope of finding a village or junction with an opened petrol station. Even when a station was found, a closed sign with a chain across the entrance gave them the unwanted answer. They were totally perplexed, disoriented and lost. The passenger did not help matters when she started to debate what day of the week it was:

"It cannot be a Sunday. It will probably open later. Why don't we just wait until the attendant arrives," she suggested to the frustrated driver, who was gnawing away desperately thinking of a way to blame his wife for their mishap. A reactive grimace and stern words were his deflecting defence until a valid sounding fault could be aired:

"We would not have been in this mess if you had paid more attention to the roadmap and not that silly children's book of poems."

"It was you that did not want to get petrol and the diversion signs were for both of us to see. Don't look at me that way."

"Rubbish. You had your head fill of those childish poems instead of paying attention to the planned route. Anyway, you have better visibility than me."

The arguing couple resumed the debate about whether or whether not it was a Sunday. They left home on a Wednesday morning, travelled all day and spent three nights in Burgundy so it must be Saturday.

"But we rested overnight before hitting the road to *Chablis*. That made it four nights," said the too helpful wife.

The car drove on. The bickering erupted again when the woman pointed out that they had been down this road before. When the driver sharply harangued her by stating that she was supposed to be the navigator, she moved on to the next subject in hand.

"I need the toilet. You will have to stop somewhere soon so I can use a restroom."

"Why didn't you go before we left," came the unhelpful advice.

"I have to go."

"It's Sunday and we are in the middle of nowhere! You will have to go into the bushes. You are not afraid of a woodpigeon?"

Disgust struck the passenger. The idea of going *au natural* did not appeal to her at all. With a bit of glee in his eyes, the driver stopped the car.

A brief examination suggested that everything appeared quiet, so innocently peaceful. When the woman reluctantly got out of the car, she noticed the drop in the temperature. All appeared unctuous from inside the heated car but once ventured out this part of France definitely felt like it had its own

microclimate as a crisp cold morning air stiffened
the joints and dampness rising from the ground
hugged her legs. The days before, the sun shone, the
air was sweat and birds sung; now the wildlife
shirked within the trees. Winter had come early or
maybe never left this place. Her round neckless
black-spotted white short sleeve top with matching
black pleated skirt was not ideal clothing. The
collarless green jacket withdrawn from the back seat
made little difference with regards to warmth but
did help her blend into the surroundings.

A foreboding premonition about this uncharted area,
uncharted as far as tourists were concerned, hit her.
Her husband broke her reverie before any fear took
hold:

"Have you taken paper with you," came an
unwanted helpful bit of advice.

She frowned at the car, trudged into a bower of
thicket, squatted with skirt up, knickers dropped
and attempted to do the business. Not used to this
stance her muscles rebelled and worsened her
unease. The female was getting far too old for this
sort of thing. With senses heightened and listening
for the slightest sound, she heard rustling in the
undergrowth as something tickled her exposed
backside while distant hounds took up the agonising
howling of a compatriot on a nearby farm. The
discomfort grew when thorns stuck into her hand
after she attempted to improve her balance by
clutching onto the thick stem of a bush. The
situation brought to mind those awful American

movies where foolish travellers ended up trapped in cellars or wood sheds to be subsequently beaten, eaten, buried alive or abandoned to die. All nonsense, but images remained buried in the subconscious to be remembered as a way to raise an alert of danger. Another random thought entered her head:

"Don't the French have a day for the dead. Was it a Celtic thing to allow spirits to roam the earth?"

Suddenly, what sounded like feet crushing on nearby low-lying branches and twigs troubled her and further increased the unease that had possessed her since leaving the perceived safety of the car. The wildlife screamed at each other in human-like tones, warning of dangers; Man was in the woods. Despite the cold, she felt clammy on top of being agitated by this unwanted predicament. She hurriedly half finished her business and shuttled back to the car, not before tearing the hem of her skirt when it had been caught in thicket.

Against her wishes, the driver refused to move until the woman fastened the seat belt. Only once this task was completed did the search for a way back to civilisation continued. Almost immediately, the car accidentally ran over what appeared to be the carcass of a dog lying in the middle of the badly rutted road. Was it moving before it was hit, did it belong to someone, were they spotted. She looked round to see if it was alive but could not tell.

Their bad luck continued as a track took them up

through a wood to only end abruptly. Surrounded by trees, some felled, roughly stacked and waiting to be moved, the churring of a well-hidden jar reached their ears. The woman held her tongue so to not give her husband an easy route to vent his anger. Twisting his head round, the stress levels mounted as the car slowly reversed, always watching for a suitable flat looking side clearing to come into view, to allow it to be turned around. At each sighting of a clearing, the driver rammed on the handbrake, got out and checked the terrain. It was a job not to be trusted to the passenger. After several attempts to find a suitable turning point, the driver was ready to reverse. Once found, the actual reversing into a natural opening was a tense affair as bracken and churned up earth could have had hidden dangers to trap a tyre or wreck the exhaust. In the end, the chunky reluctant vehicle just managed to get out of the clearing. Both expelled a sigh of relief once back on asphalt. Blood pressures dropped, statins became effective again and the driver's pacemaker resumed pulsating at its normal work rate.

"It was parky out there," surmised the driver.

"I told you it was."

Although both of them ate heartily the night before, the driver complained about suffering hunger pains. The glove apartment was accordingly opened and the contents rolled onto the dashboard to allow the driver to make a choice from the available sweets. By this time, both of them had their eyes off the road, a road hemmed in by trees and brush, which was about to sharply curve right. At the same time, the visible part of the road narrowed, as shadows pitched the bend into darkness.

Before they knew it, the road disappeared to become a ditch. The suspension jolted when the car came to its abrupt halt. The passenger managed to place a hand on the dashboard to cushion the impact while the spine of the driver jerked when the seat belt kicked in. Luckily, the ditch was not too deep for a four-wheeled drive car but someone had to get out to guide the car out, and it was not going to be the driver. Without attempting to control a harsh outburst, his judgement was loudly broadcasted:

"Not trusting you to reverse without buggering the clutch or ramming the gears into a forward position. Get out and make sure nothing is coming," wailed the annoyed driver as a spasm of pain still registered a complaint from his back.

On exiting the car, the incline and the unanticipated slippy conditions bamboozled the woman, and she fell awkwardly, covering her front in mud. To make matters worse she once again hurt the palm of her hand and jarred her elbow when she tried to cushion the fall. However, she was given no time to indulge in suffering as her whimpering was soon interrupted by a familiar voice:

"Hurry up and stop messing about," bellowed the impatient driver.

"Be quiet, you're such an irascible twit."

Her honest reply only gave her a brief moment of satisfaction. Looking up, from a lowly position, along the left-hand side bank, through a gap in the bushes, she saw in front of her what appeared to be a wigwam made out of wicker and wire mesh. To her dismay, instead of a covering of cloth, the framework was swathed with hanging aerial prey. She was confronted with a multitude of dead wood pigeons, cuckoos, woodpeckers, songbirds and swallows; some spattered with pellets and others mangled by a hard-mouthed fetch of a dog. There was even a brace of woodlarks, wrung and hung by their necks. The nearby report of a gun alerted her that the carnage was still in progress. Predators were taking advantage of the reduced foliage to wipe out local wildlife and long-distance migrants. Then, she felt eyes staring at her, bloodied eyes fixed on her from a beaming grotesque, unswerving in its observation of the distressed female.

Fear of being dragged into the thicket by merciless assailants flooded her mind. Fright took over and she let out a shriek. Her front became a complete mess as she lost balance while failing to immediately become upright by frantically stretching out her arms and bending her knees. After several tries, she finally scrambled to her feet, threw herself into the open car door and with eyes full of running tears, she shrilled:

"Drive now."

"Look at the mess you are creating."

"Just drive."

This time she had managed to temporarily stop shaking to issue a non-debatable command to reverse. The tone of her voice said it all. Years of developing a talking down attitude of superiority came in use for the ex-teacher. There were rules to be obeyed with verbal reprimands more sternly expressed with the seriousness of the transgression. The cowered driver reversed, muttering if there was an accident it was definitely her fault. The man got his wish. The rear of the car hit a concealed stump of a tree on the other bank and paintwork of the right side scraped against overhanging bushes at the corner of the sharp turn. As the maltreated vehicle drove off at speed, the head of a boar mounted on a support post of a wired fence continued to trickle blood, congealing to a ruby red resembling the colour of the local wines.

The passenger sat silently glum in the car, not rising to the bait as the driver complained about having to spend a day of his holiday cleaning out all the dirt that she was spreading about the interior of the car. Completely oblivious to the discomfort of the sodden female, who was desperately trying to re-do her face and clean her clothes with the limited resources on hand.

A flashing light drew the attention of the antagonists. The fuel gauge had reached red and it was a wing and a prayer of getting to safety. Red to the female spelt no petrol and to the driver, it implied one gallon left in the tank. At the next junction, a sign indicated a hamlet both agreed had not yet been passed, and so they took it.

"Why not, in for a penny in for a pound," grimaced the passenger.

The road took them along the bottom of a wooded valley that opened up to reveal scrubland for grazing livestock, a neat little cemetery then plots of crops surrounding a small enclave of around fifty houses. The heart of it had a small roundabout come village square for turning around, with a three-metre-high crucifix on top of a high mound of cemented stones as its centrepiece. The palladium looked excessively large for such a small commune. A suitably sized shop, garage and infant school surrounded this centrepiece. The rusty man operated petrol pump against the wall of the garage looked disused. Nothing stirred.

The car was stopped before the shrine, and a sense of uneasiness passed between the pair as they walked towards it. The outsiders were being scrutinised from behind curtains and fences. It was not the sort of place that welcomed the traveller, not even if they were cold, wet, lost, and in the case of the female, caked in mud. House doors were bolted to anyone outside the immediate family, which meant outside the commune.

At closer inspection, on top of the stones and attached to the base of the cross were a quantity of different sorts of votive offerings in various stages of deterioration, including flowers, what looked like animal skulls, handmade dolls probably of religious figures and old photographs. Underneath these gifts, some of the larger stones had been crudely chiselled in an attempt to form heads and part of the shoulders of what looked like beseeching penitents.

"Doesn't the crucifix look extraordinary large for the size of the village," queried the passenger.

The question was left unanswered.

The sound of chickens being fed drew their attention and led them to walk up a path at the side of the shop to see if help was available. Behind one of the houses, a moribund looking grey-haired crone was scattering corn towards some hens as the cock looked on. The woman politely fired a question in her best French at the peasant:

"Excuse us, can you help us, please?"

Nothing. The feeding of the hens continued unabated.

"Excuse us?"

The impolite driver rattled the wooden fence, which drew the attention of the hens forcing the peasant at last to acknowledge the presence of other human beings.

Looking up with a face that looked as if it was sucking a sour sweetie, she disclosed a do not disturb look.

"Excuse us, can you tell us where is the nearest big town?"

"Don't understand," the peasant's tone was waspish.

"What road will take us to the nearest town?"

The peasant just hung her shoulders, shook her head, expressed a closed-mouthed slight sneer and recommenced feeding the hungry hens. The frustrated outsiders walked away with the sound of a clearing throat and loud spit behind their backs.

"How peculiar," exclaimed the female when they got back to the car.

"Bloody rude. Definitely did not like us," advocated the man while turning the ignition and deciding their next move:

"Only thing to do is head further up this road and hope to see something at the top of it."

"Fine, may as well, let's hope it is not a hill of dread," came the despaired reply.

The rising winding road ate into the reserves left in the fuel tank. The pair remained silent in quiet prayer for the resumption of their urbane existence as the engine groaned and jittered. One of them was going to be proved right about the amount of petrol left as each judder from the complaining engine kept them on edge. The necessity to keep in low gear on the uphill curves caused higher petrol consumption than the driver would have liked. The narrow road enclosed by the remnants of an old wood did not seem like a path to deliverance, however, hopes rose when the forgotten radio came to life again. At the top of the hill, the mist vanished to reveal the first sight of civilisation in two stressful hours: the vineyards of France, which suggested tourist traps to give a good welcome for cash-rich visitors and access to national roads. They both sighed in relief then grinned at each other; amiability was starting to be restored. Driving on, another peasant was spotted attending his field with a strangely shaped quadruped standing by him. Both were glad to see the last of this type of Frenchman. It never occurred to any of them that the briefest of glances of this peasant for the first and last time was a visual trope for how fleeting and immaterial life was.

By the time the car reached the bottom of the other side of the hill, the couple had recovered most of their composure. When the car ran out of petrol, they had greater confidence in finding help. Their obliviousness to the damage done by the red burgundy released from smashed bottles soaking into the moulded interior carpets and the implication of a broken rear light indicator on the rest of the holiday was still to hit them.

One last dig was fired at the wife from a husband, reconfirming his clout:

"That lot back there probably don't use toilet paper either."

The wife did not respond, ignored the gibe, merely

sighed, and let him have that one.

THICK AS THIEVES

That over the hill figure in the landscape was a fellow compatriot of the dismissive early retirees. His life had taken many a singular turn to reach the stage fleetingly observed during the accident-riddled trip to the South of France. This unhurried individual was once just like any other child. Just as capable of displaying tantrums over incidents that an adult found trivial but to him were of the most important concern.

Martin was the youngest in the family by many years; a late arrival after his brother and sister, the eldest, had already approached their teens. His father married late in life after spending the best part of his youth in khaki, with the Yorkshire Foot. A Yorkshire man born and bred, named Harding, Thomas Harding, who after the war married a younger girl from *the Dales* then migrated south for work. The mother had died when Martin was only four, leaving him in the care of his father and siblings. Only hazy early memories existed of his father and almost none of his mother. The latter due to the fact she was gone and all that remained in later years was a framed picture, while the former was a traditional man and so did not take part in infant rearing tasks, which led to the son having few reminiscences, one of which when as a toddler was sliding down his leg on lazy Sunday mornings. Otherwise, the father remained a shallowly authoritative figure whose presence was felt rather than seen, a man who insisted that tea was drunk strong in their house.

Whether real or implanted by shared stories with his siblings, Martin possessed the faintest remembrance of a very early family get together on a very hot sunny day spent out in the garden. Sheltered from sweltering heat by a parasol, he was sprawled out on a rug as his mother rubbed his torso and arms with sun cream that irritated his eyes when rubbed with his sticky fingers. All the while, the sound of screaming kids and digging competed with the vacillations of cricket commentators on a radio and nearby buzzing from insects.

The role of mother fell on his sister, Betty. The young girl's housekeeping was a bit hit and miss, but the family struggled through with an unsophisticated existence. It meant that his daily wear could be unorthodox but having meals that were always agreeable to a youngster compensated for it. The sister always tried to resist the urge to touch his upper cheek and exclaim that the child was crying crocodile tears, as she easily remembered how this inference was hated. Neither did the young boy suffer too much from the soul-destroying prevalent attitude that pervaded society of automatically hitting the back of the legs of a troublesome child to get instant obedience and silence. She mostly just admonished him when misbehaviours occurred, so, overall, childhood had been good with the peaks usually coinciding with fine weather conditions.

The family occupied a three bedroom semi-detach two-storey council house with a long back garden in a quiet residential area, off a busy main road into Railhead. The brass of the letterbox, handle and keyhole of the front door always polished by the father with no hints of scratches or scrapes caused by impatient hurry or drunkenness. The linoleum floors allowed the young boy to propel his passed-me-down toy cars at high speed. The gold corgi *Aston Martin* with its missing detachable roof vroomed under the feet of his older siblings at all times of the day. His teenage brother, Adam, ribbed him by filling his head with silly nonsensical but believed stories about the world around him. Rats fathered maggots, baby rabbits were born ready cooked and all you had to do was peel their skin off and, the old classic, you toughened your hands by peeing on them. The excitement of them all gathered round the black and white TV one late evening was hardcoded in his brain, as they watched blurred pictures of the first man on the moon. However, the prevailing general impression of his childhood was that of his sister dancing and singing to boy band music from the likes of *Dave Clark Five* and *The Beatles* coming out of a screeching transistor radio with him either forced to dance along or sit in a corner after being told to be quiet.

The young Martin Harding was on the main spoilt and loved.

His earliest unsettling childhood memory came about on a shopping expedition when his sister was distracted by something. An old woman stopped him in the street and informed him that his shoelace was untied; not leaving it at that she persisted in saying to the confused looking child that it should do something about it:

"Ridiculous you should be able to tie your own shoelaces at your age?"

The nearby sister reappeared and intervened with a protective riposte:

"Bugger off you old cow."

He also remembered the excitement generated in the infant class when each and every one of them was allocated a pen pal from the other side of the world. The teacher pointed to the World map and explained where Canada was, how it was once part of the Empire and still had ties to the old country. Everyone in the class wrote an individual letter and attached a photograph to it. Only a month later, a reply addressed to him arrived back: his first letter. The writing was in block capitals and explained the background of his new friend. What amazed the child the most was the attached photo. The snugly wrapped up correspondent appeared to leap out of the image due to the paleness of the surroundings. It looked like a trick photo. Waving it at Betty, the child excitedly asked how did they do it. Rubbing the back of his head, Betty explained that the little boy was outside in the snow. It was wipe out.

Reason and sentience were acquired through family experiences. His sister was a hugging person and was only riled by him when a child's stubbornness or tiredness slowed down the shopping or the housework.

"If you do not behave, I will let the snatcher get you!"

The boggy man story was a common feature of early life to ensure the child remained obedient and weary of life outside the front door and beyond. For his sister, she was only passing on her own anxiety caused by the existence of a serial killer. An invisible killer, no face but his evil relentlessly reported in the news media: a psycho that the police were incapable of stopping. His main targets were lonely vulnerable women, the devil's candy. Demons and monsters, some deceitfully disguised in respectability, were everywhere. There was talk of girls being assaulted on the common, old men molesting boys in public toilets, and that some men and women preferred the company of their own kind.

Teenage years arrived. Girls were suddenly

interesting creatures. Some boy would always say he knew the whereabouts of a girl who would do it for a sweetie. The young naturally did not mind their own business and easily interfered in the affairs of others, especially their friends, in Martin's case, teenage friends in the shape of Jason and Steve. The boys were the *three musketeers.* All meet at St Ignatius high school, easily identified and cocooned together for being scholarship boys. They were giving the derisory nickname of bicycle clips by the others, who were ferried into school in cars by their lawyer, doctor and small business-owning parents.

It was an excellently well-funded school set in its own grounds on the eastern edge of town. Sports fields and running tracks ensured that the pupils developed healthy bodies together with cultivated minds. Cricket, rugby and country runs were high on the agenda. It was a high school run by the Jesuits to safeguard Christian values in a technological age by moulding young men to be successful and future benefactors to the Church. A charitable organisation obliged to have a small quota of disadvantaged boys in their ranks. The school prided itself in guiding suitable candidates to a religious life in the confines of the Church.

The incongruity of early friendships could only be explained by one word, youth. Fate had thrown together beings at a time in life when friendship was a priority. The core element that held them together was a rebellion against boredom. They became inseparable. A tight group of teenagers, sharp-tongued, full of mixed emotions and unfathomable to others: the school's rude boys with no interest in team sports or organised games. Steve from the property owning working-class in the north of town; Jason from the housing schemes in the west; and, of course, Martin from an outstanding thought out post-war semi-detach council estate in the south next to an affluent area handy for fast road links to up town and the countryside to the east. Happy smiling enquiring Jason was the smart one, ever-hungry Steve cunning and lanky Martin strong; possessing the perfect combination of traits to explore the emerging adult world. Parenting was a case of allowing them to roam the streets, feeding them when hungry and calling them in when it was dark and beyond a respectful hour. Their playground covered many miles around their homes. They took everything in their stride, never queried the absurdity or gravity of the situations they found themselves in; even made up their own language to prevent outsiders from knowing their intentions. Mostly, it was contrived nonsense just to annoy but keywords and phrases to signify alarm or importance came out of this boyish game.

Getting the best of education during the day, and becoming streetwise at night, they shared growing up pains together. After school, shooting off on their bikes to rendezvous around Railhead, playing at being *Eddie Kidd* in the park by jumping ditches or speeding through the town's deserted shopping centre to fly across walkway steps; all the time pushing boundaries and chancing their luck. A gang of teenage scoundrels, half believing the tales of others, and always ready to torment an early

evening drunk or holler at girls in short skirts. All
naively waiting for the day to wake up, to find they
had become adults.

In their own way, the three friends were honest to
their values. Like all the young and many grownups,
life was lived and conceived completely within their
peer group. All eager to make themselves heard but
failing to understand others. Completely ignorant of
the fact that the route to real understanding and
achievement was painful as it severely challenged
all perceived views.

Martin was the anchor, a down to earth good friend,
practical and strong. Breathtakingly down to earth,
nothing enigmatic about him with a love for the
outdoors. Born for different purposes with
irreconcilable ways at looking at the world, Jason's
intellect was respected, and it was fully understood
that this boy was not capable of hard physical effort,
and destined for a life in academia, sitting in a room
full of dusty old books. However, both trusted each
other. Steve was a different kettle of fish: a mate to
have fun with but not to rely on. Never to assume
that anything mattered to him or that friendship
would make any impact on any future decision that
could benefit him. God bless the differences in
people, as it is what made life interesting. God bless
Railhead a place to enjoy for these young fun
seekers.

For Steve and Martin as the years progressed the
school timetable no longer held any interest for
them. For this pair, the natural tendency possessed

by some of the young to want to please their teachers was left at the gates of junior school. Both stubbornly did not see the point of studying dry subjects with no everyday value. Feigning illness to skip school, the pair would amble round large high street retail shops, scampering from a bobby or security guards if their presence during school hours drew attention. Other times, they would go off fishing or entice ducks to swallow the hook by wrapping bread around it. Cheap booze was bought from a corner shop willing to disregard the law. Pitch and put was reserved for Saturday mornings, when with Jason the boys queued up and waited for their turn to cut up divots or slice balls into the unknown. Always laughing their heads off at their own incompetence and sneering behind any irate sports-mad father severely criticising at every opportunity his underachieving son's teeing ability, destroying that boy's confidence in the progress. Jason and Martin shared sandwiches with Steve, who without spending a penny, followed his friends into a shop and exited it with his pockets full.

Jason remained a star at school. Latin, literature and English criticism studies allowed him to express his gift for elucidating colourful language to explain the simple to the profound. The youngster only read the best writers, the great masters, so that his own writings would not be accidentally corrupted by any populist nonsense. He developed a serious interest in finding out the true significances of the scriptures. This bright-eyed deep thinker caught the eye of the religious education tutor, father McDermott, who encouraged the boy to look beyond the literal sense to consider the mystic and the prophetic messages. Seeing potential in the lad, he took him under his wing and advised the youngster in all things. This fair-haired man with a receding hairline and quiet intelligent face, slightly smelling of vestibule flowers was an understanding man; a natural pedagogue eager to help any child break restraining bonds imposed by an underprivileged background. Teacher and pupil would sit on old leather hardback chairs in the tutor's office, the priest's private sanctum, surrounded by glass-covered bookcases. The shelves full with old and new information for aiding the young flock and guidance on how to explain the Church's canons: bounded letters of the Holy Fathers, magisterial documentation and religious biographies about the founding fathers and great saints as well as practical guidance on writing sermons and consoling the bereaved. Jason's fledging ego was boosted by these chats with an adult.

Away from school, the behaviour of the teens was not too rambunctious. The only real criminal mischief involved a case of arson: the burning down of a security guard hut. Steve had spotted it and suggested that this would be fun. After dark, the security guard was known to sneak off home, leaving the site unprotected. It would, therefore, be easy to pour some lighter fuel against the wooden frame and watch it burn. It would warm up a cold night. Safe in the knowledge of no repercussions the trio conducted the felonious act.

They watched the flames rise into the night sky

until the sound of sirens alerted them and encouraged them to drift away into the shallows. Next day the arsonists deliberately made a detour to see if the embers were still burning away. To their surprise, another hut had appeared on the same spot and the workers were carrying out normal duties. As nothing seemed out of place, the deflated boys carried on the journey to school. Only Steve knew the real consequences of last night's action, which was an act of revenge on someone who made life hard for this youngster. The hired security guard was Steve's alcoholic and sometimes violent father that absconded at night. That morning the security guard had slipped back to the newly installed hut, completely unobservant of the switch. After being later interviewed by the site supervisor on the how his watch had gone, he was fired on the spot when it was reported that nothing of any significance had happened. Revenge, however pyrrhic, was sweet for the young Steve.

School days followed the normal course of lessons and tests. In the nature of all schools with pretentions, Wednesday was set aside for sports. By this time, Jason had dispensation from sporting activities so he could obtain private tutoring from father McDermott who had convinced the school elders that the boy's cultural interests and esoteric leanings made him an ideal candidate for life in the Church. Of course, the open-minded Jason was far too old to just accept the simple doctrine of '*Jesus loves you*', used to reassure juniors. Many a discussion with Jason centred around why there was suffering on earth. The priest reassured him that

God was distressed by it too, that God was not the cause of it, that He too felt the suffering of each and every one of us, and hoped Man would turn towards the *Light* to stop it.

"Doubt was part of the test to see if a person had the strength and belief in following the true path, which for some would lead to the calling and a life within the Church.

Ours was the true faith. Ever since the invention of the printing press, Protestants had always mistakenly aligned with science and technology, whereas we had our roots in mysticism and art. While they defaced churches, we created the baroque.

Translations of the bible and what canons should or not be included are not for us to decide. Read only the *Douay Rheims*. Its language is just as rich and comforting as the *King James Bible*.

Remember, never be an apologist, take pride in the infallibility of the Church.

Never forget that the need for ritual was very human."

Jason's what-if arguments led to firm reminders that religion was not something frivolous and obedience had to be accepted. The priest advised him to stop asking silly questions:

"You cannot expect to understand everything and must accept what exists.

God gave the races colours was a reason and he would be displeased by you suggesting that it would have been better to assign different colours to reflect the state of a person's soul so that evil could be easily spotted.

God is not democratic and has decided in his wisdom to not make everyone equal.

A vocation in the Church is not everyone's cup of tea.

There is a price to pay for every path we follow."

Nevertheless, the displeased father McDermott was never annoyed for long:

"When young, you should not worry too much about tomorrow; enjoy your lazy days of youth as time passes quicker when older. Any dread that fills your mind is only a growing pain, soon to pass. Cognitive energy should only be spent on cultivating the mind."

Jason was also advised to take up a hobby, as it was important to rest the mind and not overly tax it. His mentor declared that he relaxed by playing the piano and enjoying a swim. Young Jason, eager to please, likewise mentioned a liking for swimming.

"Well maybe, we could arrange access to the school's pool one morning before classes. It will be our little secret."

These quiet extracurricular tutoring sessions

normally ended with the priest patting Jason on the shoulder when directing him out of his room. On one occasion his hand was left a moment too long. It was a noticeably uncomfortable moment for both of them. This encounter caused the priest to reflect on his own earthly woes. Thoughts of previous swimming lessons dwelled on his mind. At the time, he was a young enthusiastic novice at a cathedral with duties that included teaching altar boys how to swim. Unfortunately, in a drunken state one of the lessons led to indiscretions. A complaint was raised and the Church administered its own interpretation of justice and mercy. A period of probation followed until deemed purified of wanton thoughts before being fully released again into the public domain. Let out after promising no more romping with juveniles, and sent to this senior school to decrease the chances of a repeat offence. However, a judicatory's idea of a safe assignment can be hellish tempting for the offender.

The unclean feelings remained. The old wounds came back to haunt him. Sporadic outbreaks of eczema being visible remainders of the corruption that lived within him; the sign of the beast: the devil's stigma. The man knew that any hint of an unauthorised rendezvous with a youngster was a big no-no. Sadly, the temptation was too much. He was weak. Teaching at an all boys' school was like leaving a kid overnight in a sweet shop:

"Female pheromones do nothing for me. I have been warned that any more digressions would land me in hot water. The diocese would be forced to

permanently send me back into a retreat.

I have resisted, resisted with all my heart. My faith is forever tested. Why must I endure this mortification? The unholy fever forever causing my blood to simmer away. The only way to survive is to suppress the emotions that define me!

Do not all males enjoy a weakness, whether that is gambling, drinking or flirting?

Priests in the past had done far worse than me. Even the secular world looks after their own. A high court judge in Westminster recently let a public school educated guardsman off with violent rape because a guilty verdict would have affected his future prospects.

Institutions are as thick as thieves. All expertly clever in a hominem manner in the way they apportion blame on the victim.

The desire to have the feeling of small hands on my genitals is too overpowering. Are not beliefs in whatever form only palliatives to help you get through life? If I have lost my vocation, with no hope for redemption, why not have fun with a boy?

No one remembers past misdemeanours. Nothing really matters. When you live long enough, you inevitably, become alone and isolated as all your peers and beliefs fade away into memory, all gone.

If Jesus came into this world to save sinners, what about the pious should they not themselves sin to obtain salvation.

Enjoy earthly pleasures, why not. Getting away with inappropriate touching is part of the thrill.

Hoping that dilating pupils did not betray arousal.

Gambling it all just for a few moments of divine pleasure."

Talk of early morning swimming with the priest reached the ears of Steve and Martin. With curiosity and suspicions stirred, they encouraged Jason to accept an invite. Their plan was to sneak in and observe. If anything underhand occurred, then assistance would quickly reach Jason. He would be perfectly safe! So, one midweek morning around seven Jason cycled into school to meet father McDermott at the sports hall. The changing rooms allowed quick access to a gym on the left and a swimming pool to the right. Steve and Martin had to wait until the early morning bathers entered the pool area, as the sound of their movements and limited places to hide made an earlier undetected entry difficult. They assumed the priest would not rush any nefarious activities, if that were his intent.

Fortunately, this assumption was a valid one. The intention was not to pounce on the boy once indoors. The priest wanted the forbidden fruit to work up a sweat first. The bathers changed into swimming shorts by discreetly finding their own space to disrobe. The smooth body, speckled with red acme spots of the boy contrasted with the hairy more muscular frame of the priest. In the eyes of this priest, Jason's developing body shone like translucent marble enriched by verdant pulsating veins.

After showering, the cleansed pair gingerly entered the pool, observing the no running signs and warnings of slippery floor tiles. The next thirty minutes were uneventful and appeared to show two swimmers keeping to respective lanes as they went up and down, changing strokes under the guidance of the man. His voice echoed off the water and walls as he explained the purpose of each type of stroke. Naturally, after thirty minutes of keeping up with the bigger, stronger instructor, Jason had run out of puff and was happy to call it a morning.

The real fun started when obliged to shower again. As Jason washed the pool water off his skin, he felt the hand of the priest patting his backside, and over the noise of the water, thought he heard the priest say something. However, it was too faint to be understood.

Jason stuttered out his inarticulate designated safety word:

"Sh...shirt-rrifter, sh...shirt-rrifter..."

Nothing.

Despite the expectancy of some sort of rude behaviour, his cries were faltering due to the actual surprise of physically being touched. Anyway, the cavalry were momentary out of earshot. The sound of a car turning up the drive had distracted Steve and Martin. The boys were currently observing a vehicle as it passed the sports hall, drove round the church at the top of the bend, and then swung down to the school buildings. It was another teacher arriving early to prepare his class. Meanwhile, heedless of the real significance of the utterances from Jason; the priest pressed his thumb into the crevasse of the boy's backside.

There was a complete disconnect in the priest's mind between the perceived reaction of the boy to his unsolicited approach and the actual one; with shock misread as excitement. As the boy's body remained taut, the man's heart trembled. Despite anything, Jason found inner strength and his true voice. This time it resonated out as clear as the bell:

"Fuckin' hell!"

 "Shirt-lifter, shirt-lifter..."

There was no doubt now in the priest's mind. This was no quivering of delight, but red mist anger.

All for one, one for all.

The boys were reunited. His cries had been finally heard. Steve and Martin rushed into the showers and pulled Jason away. They then encircled the surprised predator. Pulling the trunks of the priest down to his ankles, Steve shouted: "Look, he has a boner." The word boner echoed all around them for several seconds. The boys revolved around the disgraced man, discussing what should happen to it.

Fallen on his knees to hide his shame, the shocked priest was easily corralled and forced to endure the interrogation. Martin whacked him with a handy nearby plastic kicking board when it looked as if the priest was emboldening himself to talk his way out of the situation or make a run for it. Jason was hell bent shouting out scriptures above the din of the showers:

"Your blood guiltiness is upon you."

Steve, who had taken the plastic board from Martin, was having fun whacking the curled-up priest. The walloping kept in rhythm with the words of damnation.

"The unrighteous will not enter the kingdom of God."

Wallop.

"Terror to the evil doers."

Smack, and on it went.

"Holy Jesus, Mary and Joseph," squealed the errant priest.

Martin ushered the proceedings by keeping the priest slumped in the centre of the shower room. The pupils had become the master. Through the gaps in his fingers, the priest perceived a vision of avenging overgrown cherubs, rather than boys shrouded in mist, haze and spray from the steam and waters from the running showers.

Steve was all out for blackmailing the bastard. Exploit his shame to the full. Make the cunt suffer. He did not give one iota about what the authorities would think. Jason was still fully engaged in rich vocal insults to think about anything else. Martin thought financial retribution would make them the guilty party while reporting him was pointless, as a cover-up would immediately follow the incident. The priest would recover his sang-froid and duplicitously malign them:

"Who would they believe a priest or us?"

In the end, the pervert was kicked and told that in future he was to ensure that they had a rewarding and easy ride through his classes. Caught up in the act of dispensing street justice, Jason forgot that he was not wearing shoes and consequently fractured his big toe, but it was worth it. On the way out, Steve, who was contemptuous with the reached majority decision but went with the flow to minimise hassle, rummaged the pockets of the priest, found nothing of value to purloin, and loudly cursed the cunt for his penury:

"Stop your snivelling, you tight-fisted cock feeler."

Full of mixed emotions, the priest lay prostrated on the wet tiles. Then when he knew the boys had truly gone, he sat up with hands round his belly and rocked his head back and forth. Thoughts haemorrhaged into shattered fragments of the past, present and possible future. Never in all his life did he ever imagine that being a penitent could bring so much pleasure and release. Grovelling, he praised God for the epiphany:

"This was what the son of Lilith deserved.

Thank you, Lord. Thank you.

The agony and ecstasy of your retribution and salvation have cleansed the flesh and purified the soul.

Like the prostitute that washed *Our Saviour's* feet, the criminal on the cross and the errant son, I was lost and now I am found.

Rejoice over this repentant sinner, rejoice."

All the boys from there on freewheeled the rest of their schooldays, getting poor final exam results: the once A students settled for B and C grades; grades only good enough for acceptance at technical and art colleges. This was not seen as an impediment to Martin while the shower room incident had vindicated Steve's disregard for authority and it deterred Jason from pursuing a life in the Church. Instead, the youngster had resolved there and then to devote his energies to create art that would expostulate against the evil lying beneath modern life. The putative prodigy knew he had the talent, raw maybe, but persisting and overcoming all obstacles would harness it: posterity awaited him. He accepted that to begin with, his would be a lone voice in the wilderness, a nonconformist. The only wish was to be still alive when fame came, so his motivations could be explained, and not misinterpreted by hacks making a living out of writing introductions for great works. Otherwise, his words had to bide time until appreciated in the future.

****

Later, helping his fellow man led to a particularly painful lesson for Martin. The teenagers had by then expanded their horizons by regularly spending time up town. Railhead was becoming too small and uninspiring. One rainy late Saturday afternoon they left the bikes at home and headed out hoping to brag their way into seeing *Flesh Gordon* at a fleapit known to turn a blind eye to the underage. Unfortunately, their faces still looked too young to get past that evening's sentry. This led to several hours of wandering about until boredom forced them homewards. At a bus stop, some late teen skinheads, cladded in monkey jackets, rolled up jeans adorned with chains and sporting *Dr Martin* high length laced boots forced their way up the line and accosted an Asian at the front. When the altercation became physical with the small lone man easy meat for these thugs, with impetuosity, Martin intervened by calling them to desist. The distraction caused by this attempt to bring order permitted the preferred victim to stamper away, leaving Martin to take the full onslaught from these gnarled face thugs. After being temporarily paralysed, Steve and Jason tried to deter these feral youths with shouts and shoves but the scumbags were just too strong and heartless to be pushed on. However, the young lads' shoe shuffling, ankle flicking and cries drew attraction from further afield with effective help arriving in the shape of middle-aged men:

"Leave him alone, he's only a boy."

The intervention of a late-night Cypriot shopkeeper and some men leaving a nearby pub finally encouraged the meatheads to move on. Marching down the street the cries of "Chelsea, Chelsea" intermingled with "there was only one Butch Wilkins" filled the air.

A bruised Martin picked himself off the pavement. His reward for trying to be a Good Samaritan was a broken nose.

As the boys got older and started to envisage the time when school days would be over, the days began to drag on. Boredom and why bother attitudes became mainstream feelings. Petty needling and gamesmanship were rife. Around this time, the search for sex was finally rewarded. The boys had been fed up with the tomfoolery, teasing and pranking at their expense about their virginity and lack of familiarity with the mechanics of the opposite sex. The time had come for the talking to stop and do the do. Steve declared:

"If you cannot find within a couple of hundred yards from where you lived a silly girl to shag then you are a poof."

Three frisky young pups found that girl of easy virtue. The willing accomplice was a small blonde-haired pubescent from a comprehensive school that

had lost her virginity months earlier to spite a
nagging mother demanding that she be a good girl.
An early starter who also gave her body to boys of
her own age rather than only offer it to older ones.
The girl was persuaded to meet the lads in nearby
woodland. Martin had first go, followed by Steve
then Jason. The order democratically decided by
age, the oldest first. The girl in her purple school
uniform did not get a vote. She leaned knickerless
against a stout lime, as the boys dropped their green
trousers and gave her knee tremblers; each dying to
look at what was happening below, encouraged by
the others to hurry up while the girl groaned about
being hungry. Afterwards, she demanded her
promised cheeseburger. Being last, Steve said Jason
had to pay.

The name of the shared first conquest soon became
lost in time, along with the small wood that had
housing built on it, and the place to receive her
reward, Wendy's burger house, became a statistic in
the next recession. The only thing that any of them
would recall was that her breath continually exhaled
the flavour of the raspberry gum she chewed.

The dichotomous friends naturally had different
ideas about music and girls. Steve would listen to
anything, whereas Jason preferred the college
songsters such as *Bowie* and *Sting*. Both did not see
any point in a long-term friendship with teenage
girls. Chatting up girls hanging around chip shops
satisfied Steve while Jason, still the bookworm for
great literature, believed stirring affairs did not
start by meeting in a tawdry fast food joint.

Thereupon, it was left to Steve to satisfy the demands of any loose girl that came within his reach. After he had his way, many a dishevelled girl went home to hear her mother exclaim that they looked as if dragged through a hedge backwards. Ruffled blouses, ripped bra straps, missing buttons and entangled knickers all testified to where Steve's roaming hands and tongue had been.

Martin loved the modern commercial rock of the new wave sound of heavy metal and the original bad boys like *Black Sabbath*. He was not interested in the blues or the retrospect sounds of the likes of *Cream* and *Emerson Lake and Palmer*. The unwashed public-school musicians ignored for the clean permed hair, odour free athletic looking red brick university ones. Out of the three of them, only the broadened-out Martin was seen as good boyfriend material. So, it was no surprise that just after his sixteenth birthday, along came a girlfriend from the local neighbourhood. His green school uniform had attracted her eye. They were introduced in a corner shop when her friends nudged her into him. A dark-haired girl, who loved to spend hours on a park bench talking about how immature her friends were, as they held hands and she, tender as a cat looking for milk, rubbed her head into Martin's chest. He earned his brownie points by trooping round the shops with her. The girl only ever became serious minded when choosing her makeup. According to Steve, 'she tickled his knackers'.

Several months later, the young smoochers broke up. The superficial pairing had run its course. For

Martin, the joy of having a semi-permanent erection from cuddling had worn off, whereas she was looking for a trendy boyfriend at her school. One that she could make her girlfriends even more envious by not only mentioning boyfriend as often as possible in her monologues but also hug him in front of them in the playground or common room ideally wearing one of his tops to demonstrate to everyone that she was his item.

The older siblings at typical eligible marriage ages had found themselves willing partners, and both married for different but conventional reasons. The brother justified it by expounding that the extra income was good. The sister wanted away from the family home as she did not want to be a spinster and only be known as an unpaid fulltime helper for an ageing father. The couple's incomes allowed them to put their feet on the bottom rungs of the property ladder. No matter the epoch, the fundamentals of life were the same for most people: find a partner, get shelter and produce children.

For Martin, these changes led to more freedom to fend for himself and extra space to expand, allowed to do pretty much as he pleased so long as it was legal and did not create a mess. The absence of his sister did result in the boy becoming a bit scruffier but this was not seen as a disadvantage because along with the appearance of facial hair, it added to the rebellious look that was popular then. The ageing widower was not a handicap as father and son only regularly met at breakfast before each of them went their separate ways. His father was nonobtrusive, a self-educated man that made use of the national rollout of community libraries after the war.

Living by themselves brought his father's foibles and mannerisms more to the fore. To the young Martin the old man had the air of someone not going anywhere; just existed. From his father's viewpoint, life had forced him to learn to be patient and never to rush a job, to get it right the first time meant less hassle down the line. His shed and tools within it were proudly kept spick-and-span and it was routinely emphasised to Martin the importance of looking after tools for effective maintenance. Every day his father toured the garden, perpetually on a war footing with neighbours' cats that eventually learnt not to shit in his garden. The ex-soldier and employee of the council parks department rarely got stressed or angry and voiced his opinions whenever he got the opportunity:

"Craftsmanship will always be important lad. It allows Man to leave his mark.

Birds are a gift from God, whereas cats are the devil's retaliation.

Remember to leave some of the harvest for next year's crop, allowing nature to replenish itself."

The past and present co-existed as far as his father was concerned. The future was something not to worry about because it was out of his control. He never bore a personal grudge and atoned his brother for avoiding national service during the war:

"He did the right thing. No one really appreciated our sacrifices. Where were the rewards! It would have been better if Germany had won."

The Cenotaph was not for him. He derided the politicians, glory hunters and silly sentimentalists that placed wreaths in Whitehall. Not one to show off his medals, which lay in his sock drawer, old comrades were remembered in his own way: either sitting alone in the park or quietly over a pint. His war friends were permanently locked in his memory. He gained comfort from that while living in a world that paid lip service to the efforts of those young men, real man full of fear and ambivalence to authority. Men full of high spirits, many ultimately dying not for freedom or high-minded principles but incompetence from military planners or to fulfil the wishes of egomaniac leaders. Not only did they have to avoid the enemies' bullets, but also had to be wary of the gun happy nuts that every front-line battalion possessed. There was good and bad on each side:

"A little bit of cowardice is good for you, it keeps you alive. No such thing as a nice war. You have to do all you can to survive. We did not fight for liberty, we fought to stay alive and for you, our children.

One man's hero is another's villain. *Stalin* was more popular in my regiment than *Churchill,* simply because we all knew the track record for the latter, and only the propagated virtuous stuff about the former. It was a case of using a dog to kill a dog.

There were toffs and us, allies kept apart by rank, and only in each other's company when the rank and file boxed to provide entertainment in the officer's mess.

A victorious Germany could have been the answer. Hitler was a nut but all the same a man of the people, not a toff. A society based on one gaffer instead of thousands makes sense."

He told his son never to bite off his own nose to spite himself and to be wary of getting too comfortable. Only fouls proclaimed monotony as a sign of maturity and responsibility. Hiding behind the need for a good company pension to justify working for the same company all their life was the bastion of the non-risk-taking coward. The reward from this accomplishment was only the continuation of a mundane existence well into the twilight years. Sometimes you had to make a clean break to add some spice to life. Create your own adventure before it was too late. However, keep your happiness concealed inside you, no matter if rich or poor, there will always be unhappy people from all walks of life that resented and condemned the right of others to possess it. With a glint in his eye, he would say:

"Leave footprints of your existence.

Never forget your roots but do not make it your cross to carry, always remember to bend with the wind, think of the tree that splintered in a gale.

The most miserable of men are those that gathered

facts but never experienced the application of them.

You need memories as much as money to sustain you in old age so gather good memories when you can, but too many bad ones will haunt you.

The way to see the world in my day was to join the army and tour the Empire on slow-moving troop ships. It was the only way to escape the *Great Depression* for many of us, and as always happens economic recovery was eventually stimulated by rebuilding necessitated by the damage done in a war.

But make sure you learn a trade. It will always be something to fall back onto if things get tough and do not turn out the way you wanted.

Always remember lad you cannot run away from yourself or your past."

ON THE ROAD

The desire to pass the motorcycle test represented a convergence of all the most compelling aspirations for the young. Speed, leather and smooth shining metal cried out excitement, sex and rebellion. A motorbike was a moving billboard advertising the self-esteem of the rider, transposing everyday reality with the use of technology to live the dream. It was an openly declared statement to the world for action and not observance. Here was someone capable of facing the joy of life in the face of death.

Martin wanted the real thing. Not for him, the tinny sounding jumped up mopeds that other youths zoomed up and down on to the annoyance of pedestrians and homeowners living in quiet streets. He wanted a genuine machine. This was achieved by saving his earnings from a doomed apprenticeship at *British Telecoms* to obtain his car and motorbike licences and to buy the most powerful affordable motorbike. An apprenticeship won by demonstrating an enthusiasm and understanding of engineering through the love of motorbikes.

Martin's driving instructor was Uncle Amos, a thin bone affable muddled Caribbean Indian forever getting into mishaps with other drivers. In his professional and personal life, he had lost his way. His wife had died of heart failure next to him in bed clutching her chest as he soundly slept. Even though there may have been nothing that he could have done to help her, guilt haunted him. This human tragedy turned him into a functional alcoholic who sometimes drank with Martin in his local pub after a learning session or got his learner to stop at the off sales during it. On one unforgettable occasion, the instructor involved Martin in a fracas when after an exceptionally silly dispute with a female driver coming out of her driveway onto a side street, it was completely forgotten that the following set of instructions had sent the car back up the same street where a gargantuan irate husband confronted him. Nonetheless, Martin did eventually acquire enough road sense to get his full driving licence. By comparison, getting his motorcycle licence was a formality: less hectic and easily passed. The bike used to get a licence at seventeen years of age was a second-hand *Suzuki GS125*. A few lessons at a bike training school and many hours spent on a disused airstrip got him the experience to pass the test. Thereafter, the rookie biker used the machine to master maintenance skills and to gain riding experience in all road conditions. Jason then also conjured up the money to get a bike, whereas, Steve never bothered about any formalities, choosing instead to ride Jason's bike when the opportunity arose or hitched a lift from him.

The new riders were naturally confident and, despite limited experience, believed themselves safe on the road. It was a great time to enjoy the excitement of riding a bike for the first time as the *M25* was in the progress of being constructed. On the pretext to relieve traffic congestion into up town, it was being built to allow long-distance traffic to bypass it by circling round its perimeter. However, in practice, local traffic was forced onto it because to save costs it was constructed by building a series of new links to join heavily used local roads. For these young guys, looking for escapism, these new stretches of pristine links offered the chance to race; the opportunity to get rid of the cobwebs and lighten the mood.

Night rides were the best for atmosphere as the motorway closed in on them, and for a long time, they remembered the thrill of speeding along a new section close to *Heathrow* when it coincided with *Concorde* coming into land. The roar and the sudden bright red burst of power from this dragon shook all the senses and galvanised the eyes as it came upon them from nowhere and receded down onto the nearby runway. The triumphant bikers punched the air and gave the thumbs up while taking turns at cutting in front of each other. Their ears remained deaf all the way to their destination.

However, dramatic atmospheric settings can work the other way on the senses. One eerie night when coming back from a joyride and drink in a nearby cathedral town, they joined what appeared to be a funeral procession along a dual carriageway. It was obvious that something bad had occurred several miles on. Speeding ambulances and highway patrol cars heading down the closed off opposite lanes signalled a major incident. When shepherded off the outer lanes onto the slow moving hard shoulder, they gradually saw glimpses of the oncoming tragedy. As headlights and whirling warning lights zoomed pass, droplets of blood and splintered glass shimmered on the vacated lanes. The droplets then became trails and the splinters took on the shape of recognisable parts of a car. The final resting place of an upturned *Ford Capri* revealed the source of the debris. A car containing five youngsters, probably too self-absorbed in their own behaviour, had hit the outer lane barrier at speed, rolled and turned over, its momentum dragged it along the carriageway for several hundred yards before it finally stopped in the middle of it. All were declared dead at the scene. The emergency services were amazed that no other vehicles had been mixed up in this tragedy. At the resting spot, a makeshift line of police officers in fluorescent yellow jackets failed in the attempt to quickly move the passing vehicles on and to create a shield to hide the worse of the crash. Through the inevitable gaps in this human barrier, the curious slowed down traffic saw glimpses of some of the dead held upside down by seat belts and others mangled in the mechanical wreckage of the *Ford*.

There was no sign of jubilation when the lads rode back home that night.

Their emergence into the adult world occurred during a taxing epoch. It was the worst of times. The country was insular and dull, run by old men looking back rather than forward. The state-funded television exclusively controlled a news media obsessed with the Anglo-Saxon world with America and South Africa dominating the foreign news. There were not many placebos to alleviate the gloom. The pubs and off sales shut after ten at night and only opened for a few hours on a Sunday. Nonetheless, they were young and determined to enjoy life. They sped off in the evenings to well-known bars, some with undeserved reputations. One was a hill top hotel reportedly to have a cellar bar that served excellent real ale. When the under aged drinkers arrived they only found a dark dump, whiffing of stale beer with a bar that offered its customers cloudy sour ale. Not knowing any better, and because the disgusting looking ale was already bought, they drank it. Martin gave his opinion by involuntarily throwing up over the table. Steve just laughed his head off and Jason resolved to stick to draught lager in future. For a big lad, Martin became notorious for getting quickly intoxicated.

Closer to home, the young men hit upon a rundown hostelry on a main road to up town, a low ceiling smoke infested small bar where the independent landlord stocked the cellar with beer requested by his regulars; a concealed mecca for devout John Barleycorn aficionados. The only lighting came from

a narrow spotlight above a darts board, a dimly lit
spirits gantry and a video game machine that
illuminated the intense faces of the players. It was a
serendipitous moment for young Jason. If he had
insisted on not going in, his life may have had a
better chance of fulfilling its potential. Instead,
Martin and Steve convinced him of the higher
likelihood of being served in a tacky pub than the
trendier ones around here. The ageing teenager
swallowed his pride and put on his 'I am not
amused' face.

This was a hard-drinking world the Railhead born
boys had entered, all served by a Cornish man who
spent the working week in the South East to grind
out an existence for his family several hundred
miles away. In the daytime, the man worked in a
furniture store in town then did the evening shift,
serving real ale to the appreciative customers. The
regular heavy drinkers gathered around the
dartboard, discussing life and the Universe while
waiting for their next turn at the hockey. Mostly
northerners, some of them on the way to being
alcoholics, drug abusers and suicidal. All carried
angst and disillusionment with what adulthood
heralded to them: nothingness. Everywhere these
people went *Hotel California* mysteriously played on
the jukebox. In the words of Jason, the scene was a
discombobulating whirlpool of soul-destroying
despondency that existed to trap and suffocate any
unwary young wolverine looking for favonian
conditions.

Two of the northerners came from working-class

stock, constantly arguing about the best way to help the poor. One wanted assertive action to improve and protect communities. The other nicknamed *Attila the Hun's* right-hand man, wanted everyone to engage directly with capitalism to reap the benefits from it; to adapt and disperse from the place of their birth to maximum success and enjoy the benefits that all the asset rich classes enjoyed. It boiled down to a choice of everyone working hard together or everyone exploiting the market for their own good. The former had no money and latter never let on how to make it.

The other northerners had liberal backgrounds, grew up without severe constraints imposed on their development and knew a family protective bubble extended into adulthood and in some cases to the grave to shelter them from the worse of any economic crisis. Although sympathetic these liberal minded drinkers could never really understand how poverty and the demons it created haunted and inhibited the minds of the poor.

The differences in the regulars' attitude to darts reflected their social backgrounds. The unconcerned liberal initially nominated to captain the team was indifferent to the lack of wins and the team being rooted at the bottom of the league. He was eventually ousted from his position, replaced by a steadfast working-class alternative to be credited with raising the standard of performances and getting the star player back in form. All of which accumulated in them finishing at the dizzy height of second bottom. The most memorable home match witnessed was against the formidable league champions, famed for never losing a match. On the night, it was nick and tuck until the last hockey. The opposition knew that the last player for the home team was the rejuvenated star. With three darts in his hand with 102 required, the in-form home team player was about to release a T20-10-D16 finish when the champions accordingly resorted to their time-proven tactic to avoid defeat. Arms and legs swung everywhere. A fight was instigated to stop play, thus voiding the match.

An ever-present barstool philosopher, dour and heavy-shouldered for his years, downed large brandies topped up with the free soda water on the bar, and spoke his version of the truth, in long subjective homilies:

"If democracy is so great, why did it no last in the ancient world and does it have any future in an age when manipulation of the senses and choices is so easy.

Smarmy know it all liberals are a cancer in this country. They deny wearing blinkers like everyone else and enjoy telling everyone what they think is civilised to hear. They always act in an infuriating righteous way but so long as these wishy-washy comfortably off have the best of food, nice clothes and allowed to talk about freedom and human rights all day, they will continue to vote for the *status quo* to keep the great unwashed in their place. All the talk and demands for political change ignored when the opportunity actually arrives. It is all show. They

can always be relied on to bottle it. When there is a
real choice between political and social
augmentation, and safeguarding their own place in
society, they will choose the latter. They are base
and secretly living in horror of losing their privileges
to the workingman. Moral speeches about spreading
the joy of vocation and the self-esteem gained
through worthwhile labour usurped by the addiction
for a new car and foreign travel for themselves and
their siblings. People are all the same. They do not
mess about with their own futures and that of their
progeny. Principles are only wheeled out in
conversations. The economic markets reward them
when in search of a bargain. They seek to gentrify
proletarian housing areas only to make profit for
themselves. They are the true enemies of supporters
of both the far right and left. When the survival
gene kicks in, they revert to type and protect their
own interests. Always happy to let others make the
decisions that carrying their sins, to take the blame.

Always remember, truth cannot be ascertained in
isolation. It can only come about in human society
by consensus after examining all the facts. The
reality anyone sees is sanctioned fiction created to
maintain stability and dictate habits. Simply due to
the act of communication through a common
language and mores learnt, we all conform whether
we like it or not. Society's paradigm comes from
previous experience and conformed thinking. In
practice, the elites influence the populace by
enforcing conceptual beliefs that maintain their
power. The role of politicians and civil servants is to
promote the paradigm that sustains the system. The

media and commerce exist to justify it by creating the illusion of success. Even so-called progress supporters falsely believe that they can revisit the past with the latest methodological thinking to determine new ways of aiding Man in the technological age. The truth is that it is a rare event in human history for someone to divert the direction in which civilisation is going. All rules are based on experiences, the past not the present or expected future ones. Anyway, once someone predicts the future, it changes by going down a different path.

Thinking in this country has remained static since *William Tyndale* published the first English bible. It attempted to challenge the right of the Church and King to dictate their worldview. Even today, most of the English colloquialisms date back to his translation. The debate that existed between the right of Man to progress and obedience to the word of God's representatives on earth still rumbles on. No one has produced the knockout blow. The next big bout will be when Man creates Man with the debate becoming heated again as they discuss whether this living creature has a soul. There will be other consequences like does the creature have a right of the family and so on to keep all factions and the media stimulated.

In the end, the majority of subjects need no policing. They behave like zombies as they go about their expected daily tasks. They have been successfully indoctrinated to be proud of the state's achievements and suspicious of its distractors. Nonetheless, rules and regulations are copious in a liberal society so that a troublesome minority can be monitored and advised by an army of specialists to stop self-harming or conducting acts against the state. They are protected for their own good; told what to do to safeguard their health and safety; encouraged to live long quiet lives. Reformed behaviour rewarded beyond the norm. All because the state fears non-compliance and true free will.

The biggest lie of all is that the same high standard of living is available to all. That it can to spread about and embraced by everyone, that the young and the old can achieve limitless supply of it. Only a nuclear war would stop this ridiculous liberal myth and even then, only the literal and metaphorical cockroaches will survive. So, live your lives, expect highs and lows, and accept depression as a normal state."

Likewise, this cynic spoke about human folly, which could be summed up by some of his favourite remarks:

"Power and prestige make people believe that what they say is gospel.

Emancipators delude themselves. They want the less unfortunate to have the learning to appreciate *Shakespeare* and *Bach*, and still be satisfied to clean their houses and muck out their yards.

If you do not have to worry about spending on small buys then you are not struggling.

Everyone enjoys a good shit.

The best you can expect from liberals is sympathy.

Most people are takers, not givers.

In the end, you should put on your red shoes and dance the blues away."

Unsurprisingly evenings spent in this pub only reinforced the gloom that existed at these times.

The young men learnt nothing new, as they already knew about sophism, that history was full of men accusing others of asinine interpretations and that difficult challenges lay ahead in the whirlpool that was life. Nevertheless, the young men wondered why street philosophy with its clear straight-talking views was not taught at school rather than the dry academic nonsense.

About this time, the childhood chums' futures started to take different paths. Martin thought of escaping. Imitating the behaviour of others and living the same predicaments was not for him. He believed he had a free will to decide his own actions, no slave mentality for him. All it took was the energy to generate the necessary escape velocity to pull away. Hearing that breaking the rules led to success, Steve was ready to exploit liberal weaknesses with all attempts to humanise him doomed to failure. The foretelling of material reward for being mischievous was too much like waving a red flag in the presence of a bull. Jason just did not see the point of bothering to swim against the tide. If everyone just wanted a piece of you, why bother, so he opted for suffering any turbulence that came his way, which was destined to be plenty due to his insistence in saying what he thought, a curse that came back to inflict the old would never leave him. In brief, one of them was to become a migrating flycatcher, one a raptor and the other a territorial robin.

Meanwhile, the barstool philosopher patiently waited for the next crowd of impressionable young souls to be in earshot of him.

****

The time came for Martin to stretch his wings, to get on his bike, to search for a better life, to leave for another country. The portents were on his side. He had the means to travel, savings and being out of work, the time. Hardship forced upon him by external agents was not for him, so instead of wasting time standing in the unemployment line, this embracer of life would do something. If not now, he may never do it. Better to create his destiny regardless of the outcome from the path taken. His instincts told him that across the waters lay a better way to live.

Martin's inspiration for biking probably derived from an early love for reading motorbike magazines while waiting in a barbershop frequently visited to maintain the approved look at school. While the *Nortons* and *Triumphs* were the pride of English bikers, the innovative *Kawasaki Z* series caught his eye as all other manufacturers raced to keep up with these designs. The massive *Kawasaki Z1300* touring bike with its six water-cooled cylinders allowed the young Martin to dream about foreign travel while articles about the lives of famous stunt and racing stars enthralled him. They lived life to the full, lived the dream, and had gorgeous leather cladded girlfriends. Once free from the shackles of school, his hair never stopped above the collar or did anyone see his clean-shaven face, nor would his nose ever point in the direction he was looking, routinely broken and pushed back into position after many a mishap.

Biking offered the chance to literally move on. The quest for adventure subconsciously fuelled by the wish to escape rather than knowing where to go. If you cannot get the system to benefit you, accept it and play by its rules or get out. Transference of loyalty was the right of everyone if the place of birth was dysfunctional. He had to take his chance, could not live without trying.

Once on the road, there would be no turning back. Good-byes would have had been said and all his wealth exchanged for goods required for a long expedition to head into a world that rewarded self-reliance and common sense. Primeval forces unconsciously telling him to seek out his path. His good redundancy package resulting from cutbacks aggressively fought against by a powerful national union allowed him to acquire a nearly new *Kawasaki*: an air-cooled four-cylinder *KZ1100* that produced a lot of shove to give a ridiculous rocky top speed of one hundred and thirty miles an hour.

Martin believed if he could survive the first few weeks, overcome any homesickness then there would be hope for him. Modern life was held together by a multitude of things that were taken for granted. He would have to learn to do without social company and easy distractions like television and the radio; to develop a mindset that permitted hours spent on reflection without leading to serious thought that could bring despondency and even madness. Travel modified a person's personality; however, it did not guarantee a change for the good as any encountered adversity either toughened or broke you. The last person to notice any transformation in spirit was that individual. Some would even say going on such a rash adventure was a sign of foolhardiness.

Some early decisions probably did increase the possibility of success. The first of these was to decide to never stay overnight in a big city, as trouble was more likely due to the nature of such places, so village settings were preferable. Items packed into his saddlebags had to have a known purpose and hopefully a dual one to justify the space taken. His savings would have to be swapped for travellers' cheque and an *E111* obtained to get free medical assistance. The key was to remember to be frugal and that a roving life was not his intention.

In years to come, his adventures abroad would be retold like that of an epic exploration, speaking in hyperboles about the escape from Railhead.

On the morning of his departure, he got up, had

breakfast, washed, dressed, looked in the hallway mirror, half smiled, and with butterflies in the stomach opened the front door and left.

On and on he went, into unknown terrain with heavy thunderous skies beckoning. Hell-bent on finding an existence to satisfy his hungry soul, not running from something only heading somewhere. The effort to get there was anything but romantic. Forever on the road, he became just a distant memory in many people's mind and the thought dwelled on him that the search for a new beginning was as useless as that for the *Holy Grail*. It was hard work, dirty and dangerous; achieved only due to a mixture of the naivety of youth and inner strength engendering the incapability of envisaging any serious harm coming to him. An undertaking only realizable by someone devoid of idealism, by someone capable of looking hardship in the face; done by a person willing to see things through to the end. Nevertheless, immunity from worry was impossible but staying tough mastered it.

A thick jumper under his tight fitted black leather jacket and heavy hardwearing trousers protected by thick waterproofs were his armour. A tight scarf kept dust and insects out of the face in summer and provided some warmth in winter. The garb and outdoor living gave him the appearance of a medieval woodsman. His steed with red banding on its black casting was a bike that purred like a beloved family pet, never neglecting it, always checking it before mounting it. He knew how to coax the best out of the beautiful machine and only tuned the engine when alert, so avoiding any costly unnecessary mistake. Always alert for any sign of his worst nightmare: oil dripping on the ground or a thudding emanating from the engine.

Roadside cafes frequented by compatriot heavy vehicle drivers were avoided, as the negativity of these men concerning trying to speak in the local language was disheartening:

"Just speak English as it confuses them if you do not."

Instead, the intrepid traveller picked up phrases and words for buying everyday essentials, mimicking the locals wherever he went.

On and on he went, with no specific destination in mind, leaning towards the mystic for advice, an itching or in other words, a subjective inkling determined the direction of his wanderlust. This allowed him to cop out of serious objective reasoning that required strong planning with sound logical premises. He just put his faith in the supernatural, not the world of science. Living the moment by suppressing memories and never contemplating on the future, all of which heightened the quality of his life at this time, all enhanced by living outside of mainstream society that had the habit of condemning non-conformity and freethinking radicals. Only necessity forced him to be heedful with his limited resources. At each major road junction, the path taken was solely judged on the liking of a name. Martin Harding was obeying the idiosyncratic calling of his Dane law heritage, a true pioneer, a hero, sparsely equipped with no easy way of retreating home or calling for help if the going got too tough.

Any physical or mechanical fault had to be resolved there and then. His toolkit wrapped in cloth became a trustworthy friend. Oil filter changes were necessary inconveniences. Genuine camaraderie was offered when entering a garage for new tyres or parts. His bill always referred to him as *M. Anglais* and the likes. Admiration was never far from the faces of the mechanics when chatting with him. A chat easily started due to the mutual love of bikes. A pat on the back signalled an end to these encounters. As all eyes watched him disappear, they too dreamt of escape in search for a better life, to leave for another country.

Putting on his helmet, tightening the strap, kicking the starter, off the biker accelerated: the perfect amalgamation of man and machine. Consummation straightforwardly accomplished when an open road appeared and the throttle opened up. Each explosion within the cylinder pounded the rod into the crankshaft, producing the thrust to revolve the wheels forward.

On and on he went, driven by the awakened desires of the beast that resides in all humans. However, nature had to be respected. Winter meant grey skies, ice and snow, with dead frozen animals squashed on the road as the wind incessantly blew cold air; bracing; forcing him to pull his head down to reduce its effect. These unforgiving continental cold winds diminished his field of vision. All this made wearing of long johns and other unfashionable underclothing essential. Lightning bolts scared the shit out of him. Even at moderate speed, any drops of heavy rain or hail felt like sharp needle pricks. Sudden cloudbursts caused havoc as drivers in all lanes and at different speeds veered to the right to find safe off the road parking until the deluge abated.

A biker was not an observer but part of the environment, in direct contact with it all. His bike offered no protection from the elements and the fast-moving ground beneath the feet was an ever-present sign of possible serious jeopardy if mistakes or accidents happened. The constancy of all the features that made up the road as the bike transverse it was always felt. Splashed water on the road-soaked man and machine and tar patched bumpy roads created discomfort. Long hard days on the bike triggered backache and leg cramps, forcing him to increase his rest breaks to aid recuperation; time spent relaxing and stretching the limbs by the machine as it cooled; taking the opportunity to clean his goggles of splattered insects and rinsing out dust from his dry mouth. Emergency stops at night by the side of the road forced him to feel his way around the engine to make temporary repairs as passing vehicle headlights glared into his eyes through merciless rain. Unable to completely cleanse his hands of oil and muck, the inner gloves spoilt to become slippery thereafter. The fatigue of riding a bike all day did make sleep come easy.

On and on he went, leaving further behind the propensity of urban western man to settle for a cosy unnatural existence sustained with alcohol-fuelled talk revolving round deluded pre-eminence. Many a time, moving on quickly when the ambiance of a place was not appealing. There was no end to the open road as the tentacles of trade touched every city, town and village. The adventurer was a worthy descendant of *Ivar the Boneless*, exploring strange lands with hidden dangers and uncertainty a predictable unavoidability. Always travelling onwards, never too sure when essentials could be replenished. The next petrol station could appear round the next corner or another fifty miles down a remote road. Acknowledging to himself that without local knowledge extra care was needed: unmarked hazards like hairpin bends could emerge within seconds; worse still, hitting a low-lying mist or fog bank after descending from a higher altitude. One slip up could mean spinning off the road into hell knows what.

As expected long distant touring also made a sufficient impact on the mind, which had to stay alert and be ready to suppress any negativity that would capitulate the spirits. Knowing when to stop was key and quickly learnt, as stupidity due to exhaustion was a powerful destructive foe. Some days just wore on, an endless monotony of riding, stopping and repacking his gear. These were the days that significant conscious effort had to be made to stay alert for any misreading of the senses, constantly on guard to double check in case a lazy assumption led to fatal consequences. Forever weary of any sudden cross-gust of air from passing heavy goods vehicles or nature itself. The closer to cities and tourist hotspots, the higher chance of being stuck in traffic with exhaust fumes attacking his lungs, worse still, the inevitable tailgating and sudden braking by hyped-up or unthinking four-wheeled drivers.

Fatigue brought on by a hard day on the road compounded the efforts to find a good sheltered spot to camp. A place suitable for obtaining all that was necessary for cooking, warmth and sleep. All this accomplished on a shoestring budget and a steep learning curve for this lone traveller. Denial of a good pitch incurred travelling the next day with an empty stomach and a splitting headache, the last things needed. However, there were times when sleeping on a park bench or some other unsavoury spot was all that could be found, waking up to discover ants and other insect life feasting off his flesh or sharing his warmth. The weather was not always his friend as whining gusts of winds or flash floods ousted him from encampments. Other times the sound of guns from early morning hunters; the antics of snakes or lizards and the curiosity of cattle disturbed him. Dreadful night storms prevented any sleep at all. When sleeping outside became impossible, the bike was driven into towns to find an all-night café near its railway station, to make a coffee last as long as possible. With the place sporadically manned by a bored waiter, the only other customers would be travellers waiting for the first transport out of town and vagabonds desiring heat. On one occasional two rough sleepers were observed having sex in a cubicle. Martin made it a point to have no truck with Arab ethnic types who cruised in and out, supposedly, looking to perfect their English language skills. Instinctively suspicious when offered the opportunity to go back to someone's home to continue a discussion that these strangers initiated and to partake in some food. Instinct would take over and it was easy to follow the motto *smile at everyone, trust no one*. Food was not always of the best quality or for human consumption. Sometimes when overly worried about his spending the only meal of the day was a can of dog food.

Of course, his journey had many uplifting moments. There was the adrenaline rush, the feeling of being alive rather than just existing. The new sights, smells and sounds were all different from those at home. He learnt that the human body, particularly when young, recovered quickly and grew to expect hard effort. Although serious bikers had no need for sunshine to get them on the road, dry conditions did make travel more enjoyable. In warm days, it became a leisurely experience with many stops to partake in drink and watch the women go by, cruising rather than head down and purposely making as much distance as possible. Enjoying a cool beer with breakfast on a sunny morning would have been completely unthinkable back home. On these days, as favourite tunes ebbed and flowed in and out of his mind, two wheels were better than four. People watching was much easier as he became imperviousness from self-conscious misgivings when rubbernecking at what was around him, creating a

serene inner solitude within the middle of a busy
crowd. The opportunity for casual summer work was
also there to be had. The machine also appreciated
and responded to the better conditions. Travelling in
warm dry days allowed him to open up the throttle
to exploit the higher speed limits and the long
straight stretches of well-maintained roads. The
chrome of the bike gleaming as the road opened up
providing good visibility for miles and miles.
Exhilaration rushed through the senses as endless
minutes moving at top speed cleared the mind to
allow a state of bliss to fill the void.

The women looked more beautiful and available. In
the eyes of a young man, it was naturally assumed
that any of these exotic creatures were available if
so desired. The European gave the impression that if
he or she would be unworried at being obliged to
strip naked. Their stance would not alter in the
least. They did not need the drug-fuelled Anglo-
Saxon inspired sexual revolution to tell them to lose
inhibitions. Summer camping in authorised areas
permitted a greater opportunity to join friendly
company for a few hours. Hours spent casually
talking to other bikers, finding out the pros and cons
of their chosen steeds. Lying on the grass, enjoying
extended siestas as the world busied itself. The rays
from the sun warmed rather than blinded him. Then
imagine the surprise and joy for the late teen when
in a communal shower at a camping facility, a game
thirty-something woman invited him to share the
gushing water.

On and on he went, going south, west, east and

north, all the time observing the serene simplicity, calmness and the dreamlike world nature can bestow; soaking in the redoubtable grandeur by the side of great lakes and steer cliff faces; and travelling through never-ending forests, rich arable land, high arid plains, long curving idyllic coastlines, saltmarshes and high Rocky Mountains. Driving in a mist to then discover that a slow ascent took him above the tree line to a view looking down at distant peaks peeping out of the low-lying cloud. Never dwelling in a place for too long; always moving; searching for a new home with only the heavens above and the road in front of him for company. Zipping over bridges and watching isolated homesteads recede from the view of his rear mirrors. Passing borders many manned by scruffy guards tooting machine guns. Surprised by how many people still worked the land in the countries gone through. Everywhere there were pylons, giants that followed roads dazed by heat for miles then suddenly skipped away to lands beyond some hills, a shared gird that electrified and powered everything.

Running short of money and petrol, hirsute and dishevelled, unwashed and smelling like a hog, the searcher continued his quest. A bath and bed were a luxury soon forgotten. Stops at a laundrette allowed clothes to recoup some splendour and when the opportunity arose and without completely exposing himself washroom hot water cleansed as much invasive dust, dirt and grime as possible. After initially not recognising himself, surprised by the battle-hardened image in a mirror, his hair and beard was trimmed the best he could. Away from any modern conveniences, the thick paperback in his rucksack had a dual purpose. It helped to relax his eyes after hours of looking at the road ahead for traffic signs and possible potholes, while ripped out read pages provided paper to clean his posterior; as it was not a page-turner, his reading kept up with lavatory requirements.

Overnight travel on quieter roads allowed the nightrider to cover the maximum of distance. Days turned into weeks, weeks spread into months. Each month that passed, his credentials as a serious biker were enhanced. Then the end came. Just before a damp dawn, after a particular grilling journey through dark winding unlit roads, his quest reached its destiny, not achieved by one final last push or mystical intervention but because of human frailties. Martin was exhausted, shattered by the extra work required to maintain control and had finally reached the end of his tether. The bike preferred straight roads and became heavy and complaining when confronted with too many turns. As tiredness set in, Martin kept the manoeuvring as safe as possible; maintaining his weight through the machine no matter the turn, and only applying the brake when the front wheel had good grip. With no relief from the mesmerising central lines on the road ahead, his eyelids narrowed. Appearing out of nowhere one signpost looked like another and road markings demanded immediate attention: stop, cul-de-sac ahead. All major junctions seemed to want him to turn left. In a dreamlike state, the bike dictated its demands on him. There was no better soporific than watching road markings at night.

Having no idea where he was, it was decided to gently as possible to halt the bike and roll into scrub. There, to immediately fall into an exhaustive sleep on the rough ground: his blitz of Europe was over.

In the morning, the first thing that struck him was the heavy odour of pine enhanced by a moisture that permeated everything, including his sleeping bag. Next, the sound of what he imaged to be a deer darting into the undergrowth when it noticed his arousal from sleep reached it; followed by the sight of thousands of sparkling gems as the low sunlight scattered off dew on the grass and the needles of conifer trees. Vapour from this breath indicated a cold start to the day. He rolled out of his makeshift bed to miraculously find an immaculate off the road car park with picnic benches to allow tourists to relax and absorb the magnificence of the *Schwarzwald*. A forest, picturesque and mountainous, a land of waterfalls bounded by the rich plains of the *Rhine*, maintained by numerous spurs from this famous folklore region, a land consisting chiefly of variegated sandstone and granite, with pine forests at the lower reaches. The mountains were old, graceful and rounded by time with filtered rainwater released into the valleys below. The lurid tales popularised by the *Grimm brothers* of hauntings, violence, kidnappings, killings and the supernatural, with dwarves defending princesses against werewolves and witches seemed from another world. Nowadays all was calm, safe and unspoilt, free of discarded cans, bottles or food wrappers. Because of overhunting, it was devoid of large predators with only rare types of ravens, woodpeckers and owls around to entice the fauna lovers. The large raptors that once inhabited this land had become stuffed decorative pieces in many a front room. The inns were wonderfully stocked with excellent local beer. Its country's greatest historic thinkers had flocked to this idyllic setting to formalise progressive plans for the structuring of society.

For Martin, the picture-postcard scenery left a lasting imprint on his memory. All thoughts of being skint and lost in the middle of nowhere were displaced from his consciousness. He amusingly learnt later that the road that broke his spirit ran along a valley that was considered one of the most beautiful in Europe. His final stop was *Deutschland*; a country that the rest of the European ruling elites secretly envied for its winning economic formula: *Wirtschaftswunder*. Martin had found his spiritual home in the Black Forest, a home for the hardworking practically minded, always hungry for people willing to work hard to earn a crust. A strong work ethic was ingrained into anyone. The ashes of the late beloved were not placed in urns but hourglasses so that even they remained productive after death.

The last *Hanoverian* ruler of England wanted to emulate the German model for society. Her favourite philosophers of the day like the once much read *Robert Carlyle* pontificated the virtues of its political, legal and civic systems. Its standard of living, infrastructure, sporting achievements and manufactured products propelled it into the top league of nations. The country prided itself on its productivity with quality achieved through mutual cooperation between worker and manager engendering a national pride that fed into everything produced. It made reliable long-lasting goods and without fear of creating competition sold its tool-making machines to the rest of the world. It manufactured the motorcycles affluent riders wanted to buy and cars that the newly enriched economic migrants to the West wanted to proclaim their arrival in the promised land. All products had *Made in Germany* reassuring stamped on them. Their model for business was soon to be dismissed by visionary moneymen elsewhere that saw production as a task for third world countries, a rationale that was to drive thinking back home: let poorer countries do the least profitable tasks.

After checking the fuel gauge and shaking the bike to confirm the amount of fuel left in the tank, it was judged that there was enough left to reach a town or village down in the valley. At the next encountered junction on leaving the car park, the bike was taken left to a small enclave called *Brettengen*. Descending, the land opened in front of him to reveal a surprisingly colourful scene for the time of year. Below, the whole valley floor spread out, the hills became softer, manicured by human hand. Far west into the distance, the hills were shaped into terraced slopes. Something inexpressible knitted together the forest, hills, meadows and farms. The underworld, tradition and the present happily co-existed, creating a profound celebration of quintessence. New livestock breeds greeted his eyes: smaller than the rich pasture dwelling ones with sturdy physiques and surefooted to endure living on steeper terrain; becoming maquettes of distant cousins. The distance from the car park in the hills to the village in the valley floor must have been only about ten miles, yet, the joy that flowed through him slowed down time, and when the road allowed it, minimum use of throttle prolonged this enjoyment for as long as possible.

The spent-looking biker rolled into the outskirts of the hamlet, stopped at the entrance of an inn, peeled himself off the bike, and walked the fifty yards to a seated area and ordered a beer. His first ever glass of *Furstenberg* was a marriage made in heaven. Looking around, a grin on the face of a curious onlooker was the instant acknowledgement that he had the good fortune to meet a fellow kindred spirit. Gunnar and some biker friends had spotted him rolling into town and his bruised appearance suggested a tale or two to tell. With all the time in the world and in excellent English, these leather cladded locals asked him about his travels. The resulting chitchat informed them that this mad Englishman was in need of help and Gunnar graciously invited him to spend the day at his place to clean up and do some essential maintenance on his machine.

Instead of just spending the day, Martin stayed for several years. The blood of Yorkshire became fused with the heart of a German. Good karma replaced a bad one. The rural setting compelled its inhabitants to be relaxed about life and work hard to sustain it. Dexterity and strength inherited from ancestral wood cutters gave them strong bodies. Blessed were these rural workers for they possessed Eden on earth. The gene pool here went back many generations as mothers continued to produce children identical to their own parents. Everyone got up at sunrise in summer and the dead of the night in winter; the trademark of country folk. The cleanliness of the regional towns illustrated a communal pride. To build a village, a town or a city people had to work together in harmony, not against each other.

He had to re-adjust to living indoors again after months of being on the road. Over time, weight was regained without losing any strength, all helped by acquainting himself with the purity of the brewed ale and big hearty meaty dishes. Each district had its own brewery and traditional ways of making the likes of bread, noodles, sausages and black pudding. The prodigious appetites of the region had been noted since the days of *Tacitus*. It became apparent to Martin that by the amount of pork the locals ate culinary differences alone could explain past acrimonious relations with the Jews.

The region was known throughout Germany for its fun loving, easy going inhabitants: its cultural roots originated from southern Europe; distinctly different from the dour introverts occupying the northwest and the commercial thinking Hamburgians in the north with their English-style pronunciation of the 'st' and 'sp' consonants. The people here had a rustic sonorous tongue. Gunnar was to become a dear close friend and confidant; teaching him rudimentary German, which enabled him to get work. This openness and philanthropy were completely in contradiction to the Norse warrior origins of his name.

Martin learnt the most important rule when learning a new language: not to take yourself seriously and expect not to be understood. People do not listen; they assume strangers in daily life to speak like them. Once stopped, if the interlocutor sounds different, most people automatically switch off, as they are too busy to consciously spend time listening. If you are lucky, friends listen. He also experienced for the first time in his life real snowfall; snow that stayed on the ground for weeks; shovelled snow banked high on the side of roads, a proper winter not like the confusing mess in Railhead; a winter seen in that photograph from Canada.

Once tidier and presentable Martin was initiated into the local biking club. No hipsters or chain wielding thugs but people in the prime of life using motorbikes to reach out to the rest of Germany, touring and meeting the opposite sex at well-organised events. Nevertheless, they could not help baiting Martin for his choice of bike. It was neither an outright racer nor tourer but a compromise lacking brute force and comfort, and more importantly, it was not German.

With inexpressible joy, Martin entered his finest

honeypot period. His peak in strength and sexual prowess arrived when available girls found him appealing; girls, not ashamed of unshaven bodily hair, accepted their gender and followed traditional values; attracted to the Englishman because of his differences from the local lads, and deemed usefulness in improving their foreign language skills. This gave the young man an edge on his counterparts. With an uncomplicated taste and being amongst naturally compliant girls, Martin quenched his thirst by enjoying the best of what nature had to offer.

NOTHING STRANGE AS FOLK

Back in the old country, the grind went on
regardless of the happiness found by the migrant.
This was only to be expected as life was predicted by
experts of the day to get worse: over-population of
the planet, winters colder and the world's oil run out
by 2025. At the individual level, the fledgeling
health and environmental movements had a candid
vanguard of followers, always ready to put people off
food and drink with warnings about the long-term
effects of overused toxic insecticides and chemical
fertilizers; laments about the demise of insects to
pollinate plants and trees; and soil erosion concerns
that would lead to flooding. At least the country had
two hundred years of coal underneath its feet, and
locks-in were becoming a thing of the past as public
houses opened all day on Sundays.

The northerners and the remaining lads now drank
exclusively in Railhead. All the landlords and

takeaway establishments around the area knew
their faces and preferences. Their travelling days to
far off pubs were coming to an end. The local pubs
would suffice and become the headquarters for anti-
establishmentarian discourses, while in the chip
shops sales of *Jamaican pasties* hit the roof. An
acrimonious split between the landlord and his wife
at the pub on the road to up town closed it down and
so ended this riotous assembly. This divorce
probably saved the lives of many of the regulars as
their numbers were starting to diminish. Some had
vanished into holes to die of alcohol poisoning or
some other related illness. One was reportedly
believed to have died up town from a glue-sniffing
overdose. One, crossing a poorly lit road at night,
was run down. Another managed to get further
away than Martin: went for a walk and was last
heard to be walking across the *Hindu Kush*.

Darts was only now played for fun with most leisure
time spent around a table talking about how hard
life had become, and that the European lifestyle was
much better. State television had also turned its
back on the populist pub sport. It gave preference to
the more acceptable higher-class game of snooker.
The high and mighty decided that booze-fuelled
players be replaced by smartly dressed cocaine
snorting ones. The independent TV channel
supported by its advertisers held firmly to its
working-class entertainment values by providing
poor female pensioners with a Saturday fare of
wrestling.

The Railhead set smoked, drank and argued, perfect

distractions for the dissatisfied. Jason and Steve were never out of the pub. No pretence was made in appearing to look for work, naturally assuming that someone else would pick up the bill. Their favourite drinking haunt had a framed large Brueghel print over its fireplace. The picture was full of human comedy around the theme of a large outdoor banquet. It never failed to attract the eye to reveal some new point of interest. No matter the mood, some little depicted cameo in the painting would reflect it. Everyone wore pullovers and sported facial hair, as the predicted new ice age looked as if it had arrived early. None of them possessed the refinements required to be acceptable in polite society: all were easily intoxicated, lewd, strong-willed and opinionated. Never to develop the social skills demanded by the majority of women, looking to be entertained, taken shopping and to enjoy eating out with a well-groomed presentable boyfriend. Nonetheless, asymmetrical people rarely wore an acceptable mask, making them more interesting than the bland counterparts. Neither did egos ebbed nor flowed with perceived work status or any other artificially created symbols of success. Not one of them was perfect, all mad in their own ways.

Money was tight. Anyone seeking a loan had to arrange an interview with the local bank manager to explain the reason for it and provide evidence on how it would be paid back. Scuffles and bottle fights were a regular Saturday occurrence as football fans of all persuasions gathered at the railway station to head up town to support the designated team. Odd people were easily detected by the way they walked

around the streets talking to themselves. One such
character was a man of action, a strong but daft
looking black lad with skin that suggested his
ancestors came from the West Indies and not
straight from Africa as it looked paled probably by
inherited genes from a Scottish slave master, took it
upon himself to clean the streets of rubbish. He
spent all day picking up litter and was clearly
recognisable by the fact that the gathered litter was
pinned or tied to his person. Today, this rough
sleeper would have been hailed as a revolutionary
artist exposing society's waste, not a loony. The
Salvation Army had been driven out of pubs after a
concerted campaign by one of the northerners to
stop them from selling the *War Cry* to drunks. In
exchange for his cash instant salvation was
demanded from these uniformed temperance
campaigners. No one with pacifist convictions was
safe when his humanist had a drink in him. To these
God's soldiers, it must have appeared that his man
was running a single-handed vendetta against them,
as any pub entered there he was lying in wait.

Another of the northerners spent most of his
Saturday mornings testing new brands of lager and
beer from a large brewery wishing to expand its
range into the South. Every Saturday as he
diligently headed to the shops for essentials, the
same young woman would stop him and invite him
to partake in a testing. Three pints and a dry biscuit
later the happy fellow went on his merry way; proud
to help spread northern beers south, his feedback
was always gratefully received and given. The
possibility that the pretty girl that always looked

out for him must have fancied him passed by him.

Elsewhere, sex continued to occupy the nation, especially when there was a power cut. Each class conducted this most favourite activity in its own way. For the working class, doorways and bus shelters were heavily used. Late night drinkers went home with the hopeful expectation of fun. The sight of a girl rubbing her boyfriend's balls from behind as he opened the entrance door signalled the boy was in. Women on heat were found in the most unusual settings. A female dart player was known to offer her honour if anyone beat her at *501*. The liberal classes used newspaper ads to announce a willingness to meet like-minded couples for partner swapping opportunities. It was open knowledge that the suburbs up town were full of such ravers. Only the nation's leaders maintained a high level of dignity associated with the posts held.

The liberals among the drinkers had become house owners, turning cash into inflation-proof assets. A foolish decision made by one of them was in return for letting him sleep rough on a couch, Steve promised to maintain the back garden. In months, it became a wilderness. Death lurked in the overgrowth, home of King the biggest, furriest and meanest cat ever seen. If you wanted to know the true meaning of life and death, get a cat. No other living thing, man or dog, got in its way. In the middle of the night or day, the shrieks of birds and squeaks of mice filled the air. In his domain, no birdsong penetrated the ears. For a matter of fact, the whole town seemed to have had become a no-fly zone for the small songsters.

Beer festivals were popular and enticed the lads up town. By train and bus, the revellers would hurry off. On one memorable occasion, they went up town and crossed the river to a festival that not only promised good drinking but also had surrounding pubs renowned for great ales. The day looked promising as clear skies welcomed these autumn revellers. The only thing to remember was to catch the last night train home from up town at eleven; a long way off considering the destination was reached at the same time in the morning, opening time. The beer flowed and as usual, the drinkers got lost metaphorically and literally, arguing about which corner should have been turned to reach the next drinking mecca while debating any nonsense that entered their heads. The importance of the types of hops used to enhance flavour put at a higher level than the coal miner's strike.

A staggering amount of ale had been planned to be consumed. The warm-up drink in a pub set the proceedings off nicely. The precautionary reasoning to best have several pints of known ale prior to risking a bad start by drinking a dodgy unknown pint at the festival was applied. Some of the festival beers travelled hundreds of miles and experienced taught them that some took longer to settle than others. Although unlikely due to the early start, some barrels may just have had dregs in them.

Once at the festival, armed with event pint glasses and their left hands stamped to allow re-entry during the rest of the day, they attacked the stacked-up barrels with military precision. Firstly, the list already prepared of the ales that had to be tried was ticked off. It took about two hours to consume all of these ales. After which, they had a well-earned rest by conducting a mini pub-crawl round the neighbourhood.

Around five in the evening, festival drinking recommenced. The atmosphere had transformed since their absence. The place was packed, a rumpus, as glass waving exuberant inebriates, all slipping on reeking soaked floors, swapped best recommendations with the person next to them. Most had lost or been temporarily separated from their mates. Amongst this hubbub, stood lone female drinkers and the hired entertainers not making themselves heard or seen. The shouting of names of ales and the blind drunkenness of the criers made their presence pointless. The returned ale enthusiasts could only do one thing in the circumstance: join in.

"This ale is great."

"It's shit."

"Too sweet."

"Fuckin vinegar."

All had a great time. The hours flew by and the re-grouping at the end of the night ate into precious time. When the re-united friends finally managed to get to the exit doors, all watches indicated that with a fair wind enough time was left for a final drink at the last pub on their list, deliberately kept to the end as it was on the way back to the station for the train to take them across the river. Unfortunately, the time taken to walk the short distance, order drinks, have a toilet break and argue about the best ale drank that day did not take into account the law of drunkenness that said as time slowed down for the drinker it continued at its normal pace for the observer.

They missed the local connection that would have allowed them to catch the last train home:

"Never mind we can get a bus, they ran later."

The drunks went onto the high street and waited at a bus stop on the side of the road that by all rights should take them into the city. The time of the last bus on the timetable indicated eleven. All activity in one of the greatest cities in the world stopped at this hour. It was five minutes passed this dreaded hour. After much debate, it was decided to find a discrete place to pass the night but this turned out harder than first thought. The streets were bathed in strong street lighting and residential entrances firmly locked in this congested area. An adequate temporary shelter was thought to have been discovered, only to be quickly moved on by a policeman walking his beat. Local residents had been observed heading to flats via a frequently opened communal door. The delayed closure of the door allowed one of the northerners to stick a foot in the gap to prevent closure.

What followed was comical to the extreme. The glass frontage of the building allowed clear visibility to the lighted landings and stairways within. The decision to snuggle up under the bottom stairwell against this frontage provided the passer-by with the view of bunched up idiots asphyxiating the one that had managed to get to the corner first. His face screwed against the glass panelling. Fortunately, for this beleaguered individual, the policeman appeared and moved them on.

Back on the street, the sight of the hands of a Georgian townhouse tower clock going backwards gave them new hope. They scampered back to the bus stop expecting the earlier viewed timetable to be honoured. Nothing, then it appeared, a saviour in the shape of a double decker red bus. It ran passed them, only to stop at traffic lights, giving them time to rush on board via the open rear entrance. The bus was deserted, even these drunken fouls guessed the situation; it was out of service and heading for the depot. On the top deck, as the bus headed in the right direction, the decision was made to stay quiet and keep still. Both hopes were wrong: they could not keep quiet and the bus turned right, not the expected left at the next junction. Trepidation or the want of a quiet night kept the driver from stopping the bus and getting out of his cabin to investigate the noises above him. The journey seemed endless. The depot was an incredible long way down a never-ending main artery out of the city.

At the depot, the driver switched off his engine, left the cab, raising another false hope of at least having somewhere tolerable to see off the worse of the night. Five minutes later, every available man on the nightshift arrived to evict them off the bus, out of the depot, into the unknown. They were on the wrong side of the country on a cold early Sunday morning with only loose change in their pockets. The banks would not be open until Monday and all wore light clothing. However, Steve and Jason were in his gang of lost souls. If anyone knew how to survive and get home by not spending a penny it was these two. Three northerners made up the rest of the stranded. A northerner who was not Welsh, and two from the far north, famed for its shit beer and only played cricket to annoy the English. One had the touch of the manse about him and the other had a chin that became a cascade of beer when drunk.

Where they were could wait until dawn because shelter, heat and food were the priorities. The found shelter was a communal underground car park next to a block of flats; food was chocolate bars forced from a confectionary dispensing machine, and the heat supplied by burning twigs, old newspapers and finally everything combustible in their pockets and wallets. It was perishingly cold, uncomfortable and an excruciatingly long night. A night spent periodically crutching on knees over a small flame and walking in little circles. Steve managed to acquire a light blue navy scarf that suspiciously looked like the bed cover seen over a baby lying in its cot in a nearby ground floor flat that was passed on the way to the car park. These homeless paced the minutes away in the hope of speeding up the dawn. It was in times like this that the character of people became apparent and deep friendships could be forged or broken.

Around six on a drab morning, they emerged onto the streets to discover *Sidcup*. A place none of them had ever heard of before this adventure, with a railway station on a line that went straight to the up town station that had a link to Railhead. It was agreed to follow Steve's lead. All bought a ticket for the next stop, played dumb and sneaked off the train forty minutes later. The presumption was that at that time in the morning once within the rail network, no one would be around to query their presence. It was a good plan. By using under paths and walkways used only by porters and other railway staff, they managed to reach the Railhead platform undetected. The next part of the journey on the slow train home was negotiated by brandishing yesterday's all-day travel tickets at the collector when he made his round on the carriages, insisting that the tickets were still valid for the first train the next day. This was true but this was not the first train. With persistence and force of numbers, the collector gave in and trailed off, hoping to continue his quiet shift after telling them not to make the same mistake again. Around ten they stood outside Railhead station. Two hours from opening time with no money, it was consensually decided to wake up another northerner to get him to stand a round in the pub, and, more urgently, to provide breakfast.

From there on, Jason and Steve hung around mostly with the northerner who was not Welsh. His parents moved to Wales to raise a family but the stubborn son insisted on being English and not a Welshman who spoke with an English accent. Despite being bombed by the Irish and other irate folk, the Welsh were further down the pecking order of tolerated nationals, so this was an important distinction. The want of acceptance meant many an ex-valleys' native deliberately adopted a Southern accent when seeking advancement in the South East.

This man's generosity and constant availability for a drink were plus factors for the younger lads; a good chap for gathering knowledge about brewing, pub sports and strategies to decode obscure crossword clues. The man only wore black, except on exceedingly hot days that the South on occasions suffered, and then a light-coloured top would miraculously be adorned. Although always happy to give advice and tune string instruments for all and sundry, he himself had stopped participating in previously loved interests when life took him away to university towns and then Railhead. This heavy drinking northerner was becoming more unhinged by a job that was agonizingly boring, having to spend all day tweaking metal staves on microwave aerials to improve directivity; a defence sector job created for higher education people and effectively just a way of given them super social security payments.

****

Riding down familiar narrow streets made narrower by the abundance of parked vehicles felt strange to Martin, surreal even.

The hum of his bike, the shunt when it mounted the pavement then the clunk as it was parked in the small front garden indicated that the son was back. He would then stand outside the family home for a few moments to get his mind into focus for the expected everyday chat with his father. On meeting, his father would be extra observant, ready to decipher his son's comments. They did not hug or shake hands, just looked at each other, emotions only being expressed through their eyes. The father observed a happy strong young man, radiating rude health. There were slight deteriorations in the demeanour of the father but he still stood with a straight back and open shoulders.

His father was not overly worried by his son's absence or missed him. He led his own quiet life, spending time in his potting shed, weeding and growing his crops, nothing fancy just basic veg and fruit that looked after themselves. Partaking in Derby and Joan activities or talking to neighbours when walking the collie dog round the local park was sufficient for him to maintain contact with his peer group. The paucity of men at the club enticed many a rich widow to take an interest in him. The maturing Martin only saw advantages if his father married a rich widow. However, no amount of encouragement could get the father to alter his ways. The old man respected his past relationship with his mother and was now profoundly stuck in his ways, making do by living off his meagre state pension and some savings.

"I'm a long way passed that nonsense lad,

approaching seventy. I would have a stroke. The fact is you just made it and that was well over twenty years ago.

The dog provides all the healthy companionship I need. Anyway, it gives me the shivers seeing perfect pearl white teeth on timeworn faces."

Visits home meant seeing his siblings, friends and importantly renewal of the *E111*. Meeting his siblings involved spending the first half hour catching up on all the news before a silence fell upon the gathering. After that, there was a final period of small chit chat to inform each other that nothing else had changed: same cars, same jobs and same problems, if not getting worse especially parking. His young nephew spent his time playing with a toy that his mother deliberately made sure was brought with him. Always noncontentious and unconsciously looking to see if everyone and everything were fine, Betty's natural greeting was still to ruffle Martin's hair. She looked tired but could still display some signs of her youth when glimpsed at certain angles. Her appearance now matched that of the picture of his mother, the same dark hair and high cheekbones. This brother, heavier boned but a few inches smaller than Martin had broadened out a bit around the middle. His expanding waist was blamed on being married and having a steady settled life. His wife and him had just booked a family holiday in Florida for the beginning of September after the schools went back.

"Must be making good money if you can afford to fly

to America," chirped Martin.

His sister gave her thoughts on the status of the old man as if he was not in the room:

"Still running round after him.

Getting a bit dotty but he's doing fine.

He thinks you can get a week's shopping for a fiver. Mind you by the amount he eats, he is probably right. Anyway, I make sure there is enough in the weekly shop for him and if he wastes most of it, so be it."

According to his brother, there were exciting developments in the town centre:

"Railhead had a new Indian off Commercial Street, by all accounts it is good. We should go there while you are back."

After agreeing that Martin would call round to see them during the following few days, the siblings departed: one to get a meal ready to feed the family and the other to start his night shift. Chatting outside, they were both impressed by Martin's healthy glow and the muscles put on. He was doing fine and it showed by his countenance.

"Good for him."

Martin confined to his father that he no longer identified with his siblings. They were always too old for him, a generation apart made a big difference in the attitudes and inspirations of people. His father offered some wise reflections:

"All families have problems lad. There is baggage to endure and differences to tolerate. However, you will be surprised how your attitude can change. In later life, families tend to come together again, especially during periods of illness and bereavement.

Remember, I just paid the bills and it was Betty who brought you up, she did right by us, a mainstay before her time. Yes, she made mistakes nevertheless carried out your mum's instructions handsomely, a dutiful girl, and the kind of person that held things together.

Your sister was the one that held your hand on the first day of school and your brother taught you how to ride a bike. He made sure no one bullied you."

There was an outpouring of warmth with a pat on the back when Martin saw his old friends. In his saddlebags, there were always several bottles of the local Black Forest beer, to be shared with the northern beer drinkers and lager consuming Jason, who by this time was a heavy smoker of rollups. The suppositious writer was becoming a shadow of his earlier self. Living without purpose and becoming mentally lazy had changed him. Steve was rarely around, always gallivanting somewhere. Martin's tolerance to drink considering his improved stature was still relatively weak compared to his hardened drinking mates, but good enough to handle a few days in the bars to hear the latest machinations from Jason:

"All great writers liked to drink. Being a student of the classics is not enough. I have to experience the excesses to fully appreciate the state of mind of these people. To clarify the meaning of life and its significance required a drink."

Martin was always the most sanguine of the bunch, rarely lost his temper and took it for granted that everyone would eventually find a niche. When the guys came round to the house to drink the German pilsner, his father was surprised that the northerner, known for not being Welsh, and whom the old man referred to, while making a rapid gesticulated hand movement to his lips to signify a drunk, as 'Jug Jug' was unhappy with the opportunity that had been bestowed him.

"You work in the defence industry and do not have to clock in. You have landed on your feet here lad. No national call-up if we go to war and no pay docked.

Hope you appreciate it!

No matter what it is called nowadays, work, career or vocation, it is still labour. The state rewards some people and punishes others, and you have been rewarded while people doing filthy hard jobs pay taxes for your privileges."

These sporadic visits reconfirmed Martin's decision to leave in the first place. Things were the same, same faces, conversations, and environment.

Everyone created the impression of being stuck in their ways. His father told him that he would have been upset if there had been significant changes.

Despite the closeness of up town, there was still a distinct community spirit in Railhead:

"Lad, you would be upset if everything disappeared overnight. Unless you are a superficial person, no one likes their childhood completely eradicated in front of their eyes, no matter if they engendered good or bad memories. Every time a location or place from your childhood or adolescence disappears or alters, you die a little as your memories transform from being based on fact to imagination. Only an uncaring society bulldozes the past. We must not let the rich be the only ones to guarantee that every brick of their homes and private schools are preserved. Their heritage is a sign of their privilege and the source of their strength and confidence therefore we should demand the same, so that no one forgets about us and how we had been treated."

****

The heavy drinking northerner did not appreciate his working privileges. He had by then passed the stage of just grieving about his predicament and had entered a deep self-destruct mode. His drinking and absences from work accelerated, while no one around him was bold enough or capable of providing any help. Any hint of questioning his actions either dismissed as interfering with his right to live his own life or just tickle-tackle nonsense. In the end, no one cared enough to confront his addiction:

"He is an adult and it is his own fault if he lost his job."

"It is just amazing how the company he works for allows him to get away with it."

Wise men knew that the elixir of life should not be abused. Man could not drink so much of it without serious consequences. However, the facts were prudence was not a trait of the addict and Man self-abused when depressed. Consequently, the northerner's mental state naturally reached a breaking point. It was now not a case of something not quite right but everything was bad about his health as his detoxing organs hurt from the heavy workload. Being surrounded by willing drinking companions fuelled his problems. His employers eventually gave him three months wages and told him not to come back. With Jason and Steve in toll, this northerner went up town, spent all his time in pubs talking highfalutin nonsense until all his money ran out. When this occurred, the squalid accommodation and drink were then paid by the state. From being a well-paid taxpayer funded employee, the northerner arrived at his nadir as a benefit scrounger. It was if he wanted to see how low he could go.

Young men were known to be ruthless in their acts of recklessness and this northerner was no different. After another heavy drinking session, in the early hours of a new day, the northerner retired to his unfurnished bedroom. The provided bed was an old low-lying uncomfortable mattress without a frame covered with dirty bacteria infested sheets. The smell of nicotine and rot from unwashed clothes spread about a filthy carpet and thirty-year-old wallpaper peeling off the walls stifled the air. In this squalor, the twenty-five-year-old man dwelled on his existence. Raised by two professional parents in a grand home in a nice part of Wales, only to end up in an up town fleapit, had it really come to this?

A week before he had managed to reach the chemist just before it closed at five in the evening, his intention was to buy some razor blades. Instead, a container full of paracetamol capsules was purchased and left at the side of the mattress next to an opened half bottle of whisky used for emergency hangover cures. For several nights, the container was fingered as he stared into the darkness, sporadically illuminated by the lights of passing cars. This night, as dejection smothered him, the full bottle was swiftly swallowed as the sound of sirens and angry street voices penetrated through the draft-ridden windows. Collapsing on the mattress, the chalky taste from the dissolving tablets easily penetrated his mouth when burped up from his stomach.

Whether it was a conscious decision or an overpowering unconscious survival instinct, he rose and headed straight out of the flat, down a main road, turned right and lucky for him entered the close by emergency ward of a hospital. He wanted to live. At first, *A&E* thought it was just a case of another drunk come to waste valuable time but attitudes changed when his right hand opened to allow the empty pills container to roll on the reception desk.

"Cubicle four."

"Stomach pump now."

If the hospital were further away then he would have suffered organ failure; too late to neutralise the damaging effect on his liver of the over the counter bought drug.

As his body recovered, the northerner attempted to fool others and himself that he knew how much time he had before the damage done to his organs was irreversible but the mind cannot be deceived. The *ID* or beast within, whatever you call it, never forgives any act that tries to destroy it. Good sleep required self-forgiveness of past follies to allow peace of mind during periods of reduced sensory and physical activity. However, sleep did not come easily. His mind tormented him for his foolishness. It punished him for his failed act. A dreadful thought continually occurred: to avoid such anguish, maybe, it would have been better if the suicide attempt had succeeded. A testament to the man was that this internal struggle that did not manifest itself in any outward rudeness or excuse for such behaviour.

The quieter and a soberer man did become distant to his once good drinking companions. On top of that, the increasing squalor, no funds and the lack of entertainment were having an effect on the lads. Steve and Jason bickered more and split off on their own. Jason, as far as it was possible for him to admit it, had always liked this northerner, had looked up to him and had liked his use of vocabulary and ability to talk about many interesting topics. Therefore, without saying it, was glad that this mentor, in the end, found salvation when he met, where else in a pub, a cockney barmaid, like him, looking for escape and a fresh start. Ignoring the wise man's adage to not have kids if fucked up, as it would only pass misery onto them as well, this couple followed the conventional way to find peace of mind and to justify going off to hide away from the world.

Both the lads also wanted a better existence, which considering the current predicament was not too hard to achieve. Steve disappeared to find better pickings in another part of up town. His life was to take an unexpected turn for the better. Jason drifted back to Railhead to meet up again with the remaining northerners and to plan his next getaway. From now on, Jason only wore black as a personal tribute to the reformed friend. A disparaging attitude was solidified with the use of a condescending sense of superiority as his main defence to hide weaknesses; and to justify that it was his choice not to care about anything, to be free and to spurn the plebs:

"To succeed in life, you must emanate free will and know how to extricate yourself from invasive influences."

Literary ambitions were dismissed as bourgeois nonsense based on *A Priori* pretentions:

"Everyone is corrupted by their own point of reference where facts bend in the historical plane to obtain the preferred version of the truth."

A new drinking hole of the Railhead drinkers met the requirements of the reincarnated Jason: a pub with a beer garden overlooking a wide creepy graveyard, packed with angel and child statuettes. If you listened carefully, the cries of earthbound souls could be heard over the noise of traffic, unhappy in life and death. However, his new persona did not make the impact hoped. Railhead was becoming cosmopolitan as people migrated from up town to find affordable housing; people that wanted to be seen as special with assertive action demanded to protect their specialness. There was also an influx of displaced overseas communities due to turmoil in Africa. African Asians forced to flee when despots demanded a complete split from a colonial past, or in reality, the right to siege the land and goods of others; like the colonials had done.

The town had its first transgender, then mistook as a transvestite, that boldly went about daily life: a brave person self-obsessed about his sexuality and probably living on his own, which made it harder to think of anything else. What mental trauma and abuse this particular person suffered on the streets and around the home never crossed many people's mind; it was only the physical presence that drew attraction: a free freak show. This distraction, wearing unfashionable female clothes and heavy makeup, always seemed to be just behind Jason when in the queue at the supermarket, a queue that conspicuously created a gap of at least one metre around his person. The other queuing customers naturally preferred to eyeball this individual rather than the backwards-looking ruminating existentialist. This not only stole thunder but also made Jason uncomfortable; these new types of outsiders sent a shiver up his spine. He had a low opinion of other human beings but these new forms filled him with revulsion.

Gender issues were becoming an openly discussed topic. In a nearby town, a recently opened private hospital specialised in early and sometimes crude psychiatric and surgical amelioration for people trapped in the wrong bodies. Human rights and empathetic thinkers used their influence to welcome the androgynous being into society whereas the unenlightened preferred street language to describe them. Nevertheless, no one, when asked, knew the subjective pronoun for such persons.

Another regular sight at these emerging large supermarkets was that of old pensioners jostled to hurry up at tills. Pushed and shoved in the frantic haste to make money. These new commercial palaces did not want to encourage customers that caressed small change or tried to engage in idle chat with the till assistants. Only busy families with trollies filled with top shelf brand goods were welcomed. This new way of shopping was like an enema to Jason. The worse example mentally noted by him was a cultural clash between a pensioner and an Asian woman that looked well beyond the official retirement age herself. The shop assistant repeatedly demanded 'money' while holding out her hand, as the old lady rummaged through her bag for her purse, chatting as she went along, the complete lack of customer skills and the presumed unintentional impoliteness to the old pensioner infuriated Jason; an enigmatic reaction from someone that rarely said thank you.

From the point of view of the till assistant, she was only doing what was natural to her. Although possessing many years of experience in handling cash transactions in Africa, this Asian woman never bothered to consider the need to develop good customer interface skills. It never occurred or interested her that maybe her attitude had not helped her cause in Africa or it would not engender sympathy in her new homeland. They had owned a business there, not a dusty shack but a brick building with sufficient accommodation for all the family to live upstairs with the store downstairs facing the main street. It sold everything from sugar to wood nails. All stolen from them and replaced by a council house in a town they had never heard of six months ago. She only knew a few English words and had no intention to learn more. As far as this woman was concerned, the grandchildren could learn the language while she helped re-establish the household. If this necessitated bringing in extra income by doing part-time evening and weekend work sitting at an electronic till with eyes hurting under bright fluorescent lighting to make the products look immaculate, so be it. If she could handle the midday sun in Africa, she will endure this hellish whiteness. Outside the home, she only required a hundred or so words to get by. Small talk in English meant nothing to her as it did not make or saved money. Why should she have shown humility for the charity of shelter given to her family, they had not fallen low because of their own wrongdoing, they had pride and would rebuild. Invited to come here with no likelihood of being thrown out, they were good workers and that was precisely what this country demanded: less talk, no philosophising, and keep the cash tills ringing.

THE RETURN OF A NATIVE

Villages mattered in *Baden-Württemberg*. The people in them believed that a country was founded on the traits of its rural population, or it would fail. Idealistic beliefs were easier to embrace in a rustic setting. It was stable, had wholesomeness, and social conflict was unheard off, all because there were fewer distractions to get in the way of what really mattered. Rural people appreciated the hard labour of others and were abhorrent to wanton waste. Working on a farm or in the woods pulled the community together to enjoy an unpretentious life that was rich in many ways: clean air, nature on the doorstep and room to do what you wanted. Right and left, in front and behind lay fields, hills and woods. It was a self-sustaining world where complete peaceful solitude was only a couple of hundred metres away in any direction. One could stand in the middle of a single-track road for hours and not be obliged to move.

It was only natural that the switch in circumstances did Martin a lot of good. It invigorated the young man, opened his eyes and greatly enhanced his confidence. Knowing no different, or possessing a deep understanding of the language, everyone met was straightforwardly treated the same. Every learnt new German word brought a smile to his face. Resilience and his ability to learn came to the fore when there was useful practical information to acquire.

He registered for casual work with a local employment contractor and from one week to another did not know beforehand what had to be done to earn a wage. As qualified craftsmen and tradesmen worked beside him, his duties involved shifting timber, cutting wood, mixing cement, digging holes, stacking hay or picking seasonal fruit and vegetables. All the jobs required him to work outside in all weathers using every muscle in his body. The labour tested his metal. There was no way that he could have remained indifferent. It quickly made him decide whether he loved this land or not, and Martin loved it. It toughened him up, made him lean, blistered skin was soon replaced by a rich healthy tan and enhanced his attraction to women looking for a fun time. There was a right and wrong way to do the multitude of jobs required, and he learnt the right way to perform them to leave a good finish without crippling his body. Martin looked and felt like the happy rustic worker seen in war and political propaganda posters showing a smiling face, hair swept back, muscular man in sturdy boots, muddy breeches, a collarless shirt and rolled up sleeves.

As a lover, Martin did not let his heart rule his head. Passion and nervous emotion never overruled reason and the achievement of the goal. Martin only pursued women of his own status. In his current situation, friendships were formed with farm girls and chicks that loved motorcycling. Every experience, good and bad, was a stepping-stone. To begin with, low in the list of priorities on the traits of the conquests was chastity and sobriety. Gunnar's view of women and their needs was adopted:

"All that women really want is a good shag. Everything else is just pretence, a polite front to disguise this fact. They give in to temptation, it is in their blood to always look over the fence to see if anything better is available."

This bleak attitude did mean Martin did not suffer from bad romances and developed the belief that he was a tremendous lover, a Mr Universe.

Bad girls accepted why they were on planet Earth and got the best out of it. For the men these girls were naturally attracted too, it occasioned a lot of fun. Bad girls were better at it and eager to bang anywhere. Sometimes, some tack was required. They may have been loose but many still went home to their parents. Sneaking in and out of a lover's bedroom required dexterity as the dead of the night in the countryside meant just that. The bike had to be parked far from the house, an unlit path taken to the back of the premises then a nifty climb up to an opened window. The avoidance of such obstacle courses was the prime reason why the bikers preferred camping breaks and weekends at galas. Drinking beer, axe throwing, and nude swimming or listening to German heavy metal rock bands with the day ending with a bit of sleeping bag action. Nonetheless, when on the road, the bikers were not reckless. Transport was a necessity so losing the right to ride would have severely handicapped them. The presence of law enforcers carrying guns was an additional deterrent for Martin. Accordingly, they rode along in an orderly fashion, parked their bikes in a neat roll and entered a café to order coffee, soft drinks or just water while some of them had a required toilet break.

Away from chasing women, Martin took up Karate. Gunnar was a member of a club in a nearby town and introduced him to the martial arts. Each discipline had its own myriad of basic movements to achieve balance, power and the ability to swiftly disable aggressors by blocking blows and striking back. In essence, the *dim-mak* was at the core of all martial arts disciplines, forcing the expert to learn about human anatomy. Acupuncture and Karate striking charts had much in common. The knowledge of how to strike exposed pressure points in different holds provided a competitive advantage that could make the difference between life and death. Each strike tailor-made to take full advantage of the physiological weakness of the exposed pressure point.

All practiced movements had a systematic sequence

of blocks, punches, kicks and strikes in a variety of stances; the learning of such movements engendered great discipline, coordination and mental fortitude, and of course, enhanced physical fitness. Martin's unfortunate previous experience made him acutely aware of how damaging an upward strike on his upper lip through the nose could be. Not only did fragility make the nose easy to break but also subsequent watering eyes blurred vision and left the competitor defenceless. Starting as a white belt, the novice gradually improved and progressed through the lower ranks, eventually becoming capable of giving his friend a decent warm-up match until a rapidly executed move tumbled him to the floor, forcing him to succumb.

Martin lived this carefree for several years. To make life more convenient when there was a drought of easily available girls, a steady girlfriend to fill the void was taken on. This role required a pliable girl of good temper, willing to do what he wanted and to accept that biking came first. It was around this time that he pencilled in a candidate for a long-term relationship. It was not a case of love at first sight or being overwhelmed by her beauty. This woman from the start understood him, made him comfortable and was made of the right stuff. Frugality, knowledge of domestic affairs and most important of all industry were written on her face.

However, being no mug, it was realised that this existence could not last. Earning a better wage was imperative. Rural life had its downsides. One of the major disadvantages that befell the rural poor, stuck

at the bottom of the food chain was it took serious
money to buy land to build a home and labouring in
the countryside was not the best way to do it. It only
made sense if land was to be one day bequeathed.
Although reported by the Germans in a disparaging
tone, news had reached him of the economic miracle
back home. The sick man of Europe was out of his
sick bed and walking on crutches. The decision was
therefore made to go back, make more money than
was possible here then return to settle down.

He said his temporary good-byes, kissed all his
girlfriends and rode off with the sun on his back.
The first stop was the abodes of the northerners to
find out if there was any possibility of rooming up
with someone until back on his feet. Sharing the
family home with his father was dismissed as too
restrictive and it would make the inevitable leaving
harder. His first attempt brought no luck; there was
no room in the inn but the given recommendation to
get him off the doorstep proved fortuitous. On a
damp wet gusty night with saddlebags in hand, the
penniless Martin knocked on the door of a Good
Samaritan. Peering from a bay window of a terrace
house into the shadows, the house owner saw a large
unrecognised outline, turned silver grey by the
reflected streetlight on wet leathers. Recognition
made more difficult by the years under the bridge
and because this northerner was sober and only ever
meet Martin in the old darts haunt when drunk. The
reluctant opening of the front door revealed a tired
soaked biker and with true northern hospitality,
Martin was invited in.

There were noticeable differences in the country that the biker could not remain ignorant for long. The pleasant green fields of England were now covered in yellow. In town, extra vigilance was required when travelling about due to slapdash digging and the overuse of tarmac to refill holes in lieu of restoring roads and pavements with original materials. The smell of gas due the continual digging was so apparent that it was amazing that few people mentioned it. It had just become a normally expected smell. In addition, the language on the streets was initially hard to fathom as the locals were continually asking questions of him by emphasising the last word in their sentences. The arrival of cable TV and the popularity of Australian soaps later explained these bizarrely accepted nuisances. Another significant life changing development was the arrival of credit cards and hole in the wall cash machine to feed the growing consumer driven economy. Mind, some things had not changed. The traditional workingman's essentials were still extortionately expensive with considerable price increases observed in beer and petrol leading the way. Deemed pariahs, it was as if someone did not like the habits of the lower classes. There was still nowhere that sold a good cup of coffee but the chance to drink strong tea again was appreciated.

It did not take him long to make use of a permanent address. The siblings were alerted of his return, he signed on at the job centre and more importantly registered with employment agencies on the high street. A job at an in-house supermarket bakery was about to be accepted when the first unemployment payment cheque put a halt to this proposal. It turned out that under German unemployment laws the unemployed were entitled to two-thirds of their previous pay. It was irrelevant where it was claimed, as all European countries had reciprocated agreements. The German authorities calculated the correct payment in Deutschmarks and informed the local employment office in Railhead of the amount. This office subsequently authorised the payment without considering exchange rates. Martin could not believe his eyes when his mail was opened and saw the amount on the cheque, nor could the northerner now be wishing that he had charged him the going rate for rent.

"Shit!"

The pair looked at the amount and rolled their eyes in disbelief.

"Just imagine how much dole money you would have got if you had spent the last few years working in Italy and was paid in Lire," conjectured the northerner.

"Surely this type of mistake in the payment is too blatant?"

"Maybe not, payments are probably computerised and it looks as if there is no currency exchange rate routine in the program. Unless someone complains about getting too much, they will never know."

In case it was a mistake, the cheque was quickly

cashed. However, the same amount arrived without fail every fortnight for a year.

Not only did Martin manage to save money but also could afford to regularly ride out to the Black Forest to reacquaint himself with good countryside living, and return with some alcoholic goodies for his landlord, whose depression about the unfairness in life had significantly deepened.

The conscientious biker made time to completely refurbish the bike, a task reluctant to do in Germany, as his everyday German did not extend sufficiently into its technical language. Now safe in the knowledge that he knew the name of every part and where to get any replacements, it was stripped down and completely rebuilt. The dismantled parts methodically spread out in the backyard with decisions made on which to keep and refresh by a good oiling or greasing and those to replace. It was a labour of love. The northerner did not appreciate this messy affair as no matter how hard the biker tried, oil left its mark. However, Martin's strength came in handy when help was required to lug goods and furnishings. For the house owner, crippling mortgage repayments left little cash left at the end of the month so instead of hiring expensive and hopefully competent tradesmen, arduous participation in the new national craze of *DIY* was necessitated.

Jason was rarely seen around this time and Steve was long gone. At first, on eventually meeting Jason, what was seen and heard surprised Martin. It was initially assumed it was only the sharp contrast between countryside prosaic behaviour and the reacquaintance with someone with a quick mind. However, there was an added harshness in the speech of his friend, who was unnecessary opining and rude in a disparagingly pompous way. Underneath it all, it was still Jason but with a boosted eccentricity. This was easily accepted, as in his way, Martin felt more superior and worldly wise than the locals. His travels had turned him from a boy into the man. Nevertheless, the resultant hug when the friends first met reflected the contrast recent life had made on them. Martin lifted Jason in the air with ease and at close range noticed that his friend had broadened out, especially around the neck. His skin also had that unhealthy murky sheen that chain smokers and heavy drinkers developed.

The northerners told Martin that Steve was enjoying life up town as a paid artist.

 "Yes, he was an artist!"

Steve had found a milieu that suited his requirements and the Railhead gang would sometimes be invited up town to view the latest exhibition of his cooperative's work or just bum about his haunts.

"It was always a good laugh and worth the hangover."

Martin found it difficult to make the effort to keep fit. Without a fellow comrade to encourage and motivate him, his enthusiasm waned. An evening was spent at a Karate school but the experience dissuaded him to join due to the type of person the place attracted. Karate was supposed to be a character building activity as well as a method of defence. Unfortunately, the Dan running the school had let that side of it slip. For Martin, it led to a painful lesson as a thuggish element took full advantage of the obvious discrepancy in the belt classifications between the two countries. Instead of ceasing when the unfair superiority became apparent, the thugs enjoyed a bit of sadistic fun. Back at the house, bloodied, black eyed with a nose further out of joint, it was suggested to the beleaguered northerner that in future they could practice some moves. The evidence in front of this not so daft man persuaded him to decline this kind offer. Shortly, Martin's interest in attempting to preserve his fitness diminished completely when he got a good job that enabled him to invite his German girlfriend to come over and buy a flat of their own. An affordable flat considerably out of Railhead using a deposit paid with the life savings of the girl.

Meanwhile, his father was still the same, plodding along with the dog by his side. Betty's kids were all at school and his brother's wife was expecting a second child. This brother strongly suggested that once Martin was re-established, marriage should be considered, as it was sensible to do so at his age, and importantly the tax breaks were excellent. Another outcome of the reunion with his sibling was it resulted in the good blue-collar job via Adam's efforts. The company his brother worked for preferred to hire workers recommended by recognised reliable employees, as the management believed that this improved the chances of hiring someone that was just as reliable and not afraid of long hours. The last thing this company could afford was any disruption to the production lines; disruption cut profit. An interview was arranged and Martin passed with flying colours. His 'I will do anything' attitude and recent experiences went down well. The interview was so successful that, instead of starting at the bottom, he was immediately made a member of a key crew that attracted the jealousy of other workers due to the potential earnings available to this privileged team.

Martin had to commute to the edge of up town through Railhead and the main road that passed near his father's home. His new employers were the largest manufacturers of photographic film in Europe. Plastic sheets were sprayed with various gelatine emulsions, cut to the correct size, spooled onto lightproof reels and appropriately labelled and packaged for the region to be sold. Each manufacturer had copyrighted colour production techniques, which were heavily branded as the best ever. It was a sought after, cheap to mass-produce product that marketing departments spent a fortune on advertising to keep its name in the minds of the customers. Martin role was to ensure production ran smoothly, that the emulsion vessels never fell below critical levels and that the spray guns, cutters and rollers continually ran within acceptable tolerances. Any issues within his field of vision that could affect the quality of the product or stop production had to be immediately reported. No matter how intensely a product was promoted if the quality became poor and better alternatives existed then customers showed no loyalty.

Martin quickly earned the trust of his shift manager and a bonus payment was soon awarded when a cost-effective remote mechanical alert was suggested, based on the toilet flush system, to flip up a warning indicator flag when a connected float lost contact with the emulsion fluids in the large vessels. This simple and cheap innovation removed the need to have someone dedicated to continually check each vessel. The idea came to him while spending a day observing a technical services consultant trying to find the optimum positions to place a set of expensive lasers to correctly detect the minimum permissible fluid level before a refill was required.

His girlfriend was several years younger than Martin, around eighteen, a shortish curly blond-haired girl with a nice rounded bum perfect for sitting on the back of a bike, with a nature that was the embodiment of kindness, compassion and the making of a good mother. Nevertheless, in Martin's eyes, she was not the one: too dependent on him. Shyness and lack of confidence in her new surroundings prevented complete integration to allow her to contribute to the budget. On the plus side, her presence did allow him to dip his wick while waiting for something better to come along.

His father did not help matters when he first met

the young girl by recounting old war stories and the fact that he knew many German girls after the war when based there during the early days of the occupation:

"All you needed were fags and chocolate…"

Betty interrupted him before what was received in return was verbally expressed.

"No more whisky for you."

"Ridiculous, ruled at home and in the country by a woman."

When not working, the couple were regularly invited round for dinner and family night outs with photographs taken alongside nephews and nieces. The siblings and the couple sampled many a good meal at new restaurants that were popping up all other the place. Betty took a liking to the girl and did all that was possible to help her settle. She made an effort to make the girl comfortable, get to know the area and to acclimatise the girl to her new life. She would drive out to the flat, take her shopping and visit known beauty spots. The girl was told where and where not to shop for essentials. Some of the quaint and illogical local customs were explained to her. The women even used public transport to familiarise the newcomer with routes to towns within reasonable reach. This mentoring illustrated to Betty how much she took for granted and how dependent everyone was on the help of others.

"What was the point of her swapping one village for

just another one. She had to get some benefit of
being in another country and not just hang about a
flat all day."

The pair grew to like each other with Betty
naturally taking a motherly role to bring the girl out
of herself. What struck the German girl most was
the taking for granted of the lack of local products in
the shops and the cramp living accommodations.
The ceilings were barely above head height, amply
proven by her ability to almost touch the ceilings by
just stretching out her arm. Similarly, Betty was
surprised how young the German was and expressed
her view that it was a brave thing to come all this
way. She would not have had the nerve to do it and
reflected that the girl must really like her young
sibling. It must also be worrying for her family in
Germany that she was so far away.

All who met her liked the young German, who did
not have a bad bone in her body. Consequently, the
breakup came as a sudden surprise and was queried
by his siblings. The northern friends only found out
about the split over a game of snooker when the
news came from the girl. She informed one of them
while Martin was at the table that the pair were
parting. It was expressed with a sad finality that
suggested it was not her decision. That was the last
time the girl was seen. Later a northerner thought
that the decision was probably predetermined long
ago by recalling the day Martin came round to see
how things were going and wondered if he fancied a
quick pint. On the way to the pub, Martin expressed
the need to buy the girl a birthday present. Stopping

at a jeweller, the pair looked into the window, the front was mainly filled with displays of rings of all sorts. Martin voiced the opinion that was the last thing to buy, as it would create false hopes.

Betty raised her head about the parapet to query the logic behind the breakup:

"What are you expecting from the girl," proclaimed a puzzled Betty.

"She was sweet and prepared to set up a home with you, and you tell her to pack her bags and go because it was not to your expectations. She was barely out of school. It was up to you to be tolerant and accept she had a learning curve. It is hard enough to set up home when you are that age but to do it in another country without the support of your parents or family members that is a hard task."

Martin was not completely ruthless. The girl got back the deposit with some interest, not matching the value seen in the rise in house prices that had occurred, but a small increase nevertheless. A fortnight later Freddi arrived. This replacement was five years older than the displaced girl. She was the one pencilled in as a long-term partner. Within a couple of months, they had married. A quiet ceremony and reception conducted over a sunny weekend in the presence of a few friends, ending on Monday when the pair returned to work.

Freddi was the sort of practical wife a sensible man desired. She was no frivolous doddle, quite the opposite: prudent spender, house proud and generous with her portions at meal times. A woman Martin could rely on through thick and thin times. She had the look of a sturdy milkmaid about her, built to work. Her black hair usually was French braided, allowing it to be pinned high while working and hung loosely when socialising. Their relationship was a practical decision between them. She had not fuelled his passions and him, not hers. Both were approaching an age for marrying and had agreed to meet up again when current relationships had run the course. Both were not sentimental and never dwelled on feelings for previous lovers. It was not a case of love but common sense; the couple suited each other and could trust the other to commit to the hope of achieving financial security quickly. This last desire was what held them together, a common goal to raise money to allow them to live comfortably in their bucolic Eden. Every creature dreams, reflexive twitching betrays the nature of these dreams. The cat outwits and pounces on a large intelligent bird like a magpie. The dog snatches a rabbit before it gets down its burrow. Man escapes from drudgery. Only Man seemed capable of using dreams to sustain a pursuit to achieve his aims.

It all augured well as it only rained good fortune on the newlyweds.

SUNSHINE OVER RAILHEAD

In the USA, a financial guru believed the current
Prime Minister, basking in the halo effect due to a
rise in national spirit from an inadvertent military
conflict, was someone that could be useful to
expedite his business interests. The decision was
made to support her. In an arranged private
meeting, an audacious strategy to solidify her
position was presented. Her government must
promote a formula, which embraced a specific type
of postmodern national identity: one based on self-
reliance and unconcern for others. It was pointed out
that the success of great hubs like *New York* and
San Francisco was based on the encouragement of
individual free expression to nurture
entrepreneurial spirit and maximise wealth
creation. The American Midwest complained about
the morals and behaviour in such places but at the

end of the day, the financial rewards that these hubs created were wholeheartedly accepted.

Over a quiet one-to-one lunch, the guru fired up her interest in his proposed adventure with a rousing pep talk:

"Be audacious. Promote the free market and invite the world to compete for your services. Greater individualism is the key to winning the race to influence the shape of globalisation. Free the entrepreneurs and they will encourage others to follow. Just wrap the national flag around you and declare anyone that disagrees as an enemy of the state. People have short memories, accept authority and essentially spend their lives obeying rules dictated to them. The secret of successful control is to allow the free market to create distractions and role models that produce citizens that copycat desirable traits. Traits that allow the state to govern without organised interference.

If you want rapid progress, get rid of moral influences preaching interdependency and one nation nonsense. Be a radical liberal, hijack your party and turn it away from traditional conservative values. Deregulate everything. Let new ideas flourish without state intervention. Invite the best talent from the world to come to force everyone to compete. Allow foreign producers to supply all the goods in a consumer-driven market so that these countries become dependent on your purchases so giving your country unlimited international credit to continually buy their goods.

Squash the old preoccupation of the fear of household debt. The new economic paradigm demands the embracement of credit and debt as friends. Let the market enrich itself with easy money.

It is a win-win formula as future progeny will go on and create their own little enterprises to provide even more consumer services so creating a never-ending spiral of success."

The new advisor even volunteered an improvement to her image:

"Therefore, go on out there and soften them up, prepare them for change; and do something about your hair, it is so not now, never has been since the early fifties."

This conversion to radical neo-liberalism signified good tidings for the South: boom time. Welcome to the new age. With complete implacability, out of date values were dismissed. Lucrative deals were made to release state wealth and services to right minded global businessmen. The profits of marketing companies soared. The message was made clear: a society had to continually renew its possessions to allow advancements to be made; otherwise, the world would just come to a standstill. The old supposition that the number of reliable borrowers should always significantly outnumber those that could not meet repayments for chaotic or mischievous reasons was ignored. Credit was made available to everyone.

Money grabbing was all the rage and all and sundry became entrepreneurs. Car boot sales replaced giving unwanted goods to charity. Why waste anything when you could make a few bob by standing outside in a freezing or wet car park. Church leaders dismissed as old men in flocks when it was preached that the unbridled show of luxury was a deadly sin. Barrow boys competed with private school chums. Owners of the same foreign sports cars hooted at each other as a recognition of being in the same exclusive club. The celebrity craze rocketed into the stratosphere as every schoolboy and girl were discouraged from being a scientist or engineer, but instead just go out and obtain the cornucopia of rewards that awaited them by becoming an overnight someone. Easy credit led to house price inflation. At international summits, the government ministers boasted that the South East had been turned into the largest complex of office blocks in the world where workers not only worked the longest hours but also had the most time-consuming commuting journeys. Estate agents, beamed money grins, as they rushed around knocking on doors pestering owners to sell their property and encouraging council tenants to buy rented property. It did not matter if people supported the government or not, had been a loyal paid up member of society, a layabout or just off the boat, a mortgage could be found if a council house was considered desirable and possible to sale on, even the almshouses were sold off. Exorbitant extravagance became commonplace as the South became a nation of paper millionaires. The top champagne-drinking region in the world with Red

Porsche sports cars nonchalantly parked on every street and the *Beaujolais nouveau* run an annual media covered event. Even better news was the end of new ice age predictions as higher consumption and easier foreign travel meant the Earth would get hotter so preventing this unwanted catastrophe.

Thank God for unbridled global capitalism.

Jason and Martin both became followers of the new way but from a different outlook; one fully embraced debt and the other endeavoured to acquire assets using the available credit. The pragmatic Martin grasped the potential of returning to Germany quicker than ever dreamt. However, both were happy to be closed minded, indifferent to the community and life beyond it. Jason became chipper when his credit cards arrived in the post. Never ever felt welcomed in a credit-controlled world, he was proud to be given the role of the consumer without fully understanding the subtly of why spending helped the economy but was happy to do his bit. It had something to do with the fact that it had worked out because the country was going to be richer in the future then it allowed everyone to start spending more now. In life, there were winners and losers, and the West enjoyed cheap goods made in the third world.

At the same time, Freddi worked hard to establish herself: initially gaining useful employment in a nearby CO-OP convenience shop before getting a permanent office position at a plastic sheet company, which produced coloured and moulded displays for the ever-expanding and changing high street shops. She staffed the phones and took orders from all over the country. The natives were a continual source of amusement to her. Through her working experiences, she found them silly, prepared to eat anything and possessing pompous ideas. A pretentious graduate in her office was forever a source of bewilderment to her:

"He comes in every morning and spends an hour reading the *FT* before starting the same job as me!"

For the married couple, life was a race to accumulate wealth, sacrificing their prime years to do so. The fact was it was a rewarding time to conform, play your cards right in an epoch favourable for the moneymen. Martin had strong allies to support him, as two women fought hard for his betterment; one was his ever-present wife and the other a political leader not tolerating any interference to profit making. His only flaw continued to be the inherent proneness to not being able to handle his drink, especially when tired. One moment everything appeared fine, the next he was rolling on the ground gibbering like a happily contented fool.

Freddi kept a nice home and was always welcoming to Martin's friends; never tempted to split him away from previous acquaintances or attempted to reshape him. All that she demanded was stamina, stamina to work hard, earn money, be industrious, act like a good German, and, of course, provide a lovemaking role as well; working hard and sex kept a wife happy. Anything else would be a sign of ingratitude for her good efforts. She also had an excellent shepherding instinct when it came to rounding up the drunks after a pub session to make sure everyone got home safely. It was her love-chore for her rarely chastised husband, and that was only done in private.

Nonetheless, she, for the life of her, could not make out Jason. In her world, Martin was good and Jason bad, the hard worker and the shirker. It was a strange fact that outright materialistic beings and those seeking a more leisurely life experience rarely shared any middle ground; simply put each did not understand the other. Their internal clocks ran at different speeds, she was always a five minutes early person while Jason arrived any time after the agreed appointment. She dreaded time wasting and the other dreaded losing his free time by being forced to march to someone else's drumbeat. If lucky, an existence of four score and seven years was contracted to a human being. Free radicals surmised that given the Universe was thirteen billion years old and the Earth was five billion years in the making, with several billion to go if nature had its way and probably only a century if Man had his, then why bother. Materialists took the opposite viewpoint. They must make the best of it and acquire riches. Martin found himself in the middle ground. On one side, his wife was one hundred percent focused on the rewards and Jason always available for socialising. A part of him wanted the same relaxed existence as Jason while another part fully understood the future gains to be had by committing to work hard.

Freddi being a foreigner did understand the northern friends better and spoke to many northerners over the phone at work, picking up antiquated phrases as the men at the over end teased her. When it was pointed out that the men were flirting with her, the affronted woman would stoutly refute any unfaithful behaviour:

"I do not flirt with them. I am working."

It was not all good times. After a rapid decline in health Martin's father died. In his coffin, the old soldier looked smaller, different and smelt wrong. At the funeral, the family gathered round:

"The cancer got him but it was pneumonia that finished him."

"They think working with pesticides that did it."

"It is everywhere in the food chain nowadays, causes miscarriages and everything."

"They say these new cell phones cause cancer of the inner ear."

"If nothing else does then cancer gets you in the end."

"You wouldn't leave the house if you worried about all the things people say."

At the reception, talk revolved round the old man's

habits and beliefs. Betty informed Martin that when a child the last thing at night father would check that he was sound asleep and well wrapped up before turning the landing light off.

"He would not have liked what is going on now," claimed the sister.

"We need good public services like hospitals and schools. Only a man would think these things unimportant whereas we women know that when nature calls these are essentials for our safety and the development of our children.

As a mum, it is obvious that people develop differently and in their own way contribute, so rewarding some and not others is simply vindictive."

Martin found out at the reception from distant cousins, who came down from Yorkshire to represent their families, that before coming down south, his father was a lamplighter in his youth. This revelation came out of happy reminiscences of the families' past and how they had fared. It had never occurred to him that pea soupers, rickets and children running around without shoes were recent history that had affected his parents and not Victorian horrors incessantly described by *Charles Dickens*. It had been hard filthy labour for his parents' generation. His false image of life had been shaped by the films of the day: heroic Americans defeating nasty enemies, hippies and the rich living in glamorous houses. Afterwards, Martin headed into town to drag the northerners out for a drink.

With no mention of the funeral, he got plastered.

After the funeral, the purchase of the council house came to light. No one knew that Martin had convinced the frail father to allow him to buy the heavily discounted council house under his name and to write a will leaving it all to him. The first time the new owner entered the vacant house it felt as if he was trespassing; a chill and strangeness hit him. Before inviting a house clearance agent to value the contents, Martin conducted a search of the place and was surprised by what was discovered: a small fortune was found hidden away all over the house. Money was hidden in socks, pots and in a battered suitcase under the bed. His father must have been saving up for his funeral for years. The house clearance agent would have loved to have found this cash first but in the end settled for a few small items that made it into the bric-a-brac category.

The other siblings were incensed that everything was sieged without any consultation. Not only that the dog was put down and all the possessions that remained, after the house clearance agent took what was thought resalable, were quickly thrown in a skip. Needless to say, the relationship with the rest of the family suffered irrevocable damage. His brother turned his back on him and opted for different work shifts while Betty was dismayed and decided to have strong words with him about family values and doing the right thing. It was a palaver she could do without but compulsion drove her to have her say. She turned up at the doorstep of the purchased house to chide and harry him for his greed and lack of thought. To keep emotions to a minimum she averted her face while she gave verbal expression to her exasperation:

"What wilfulness have we done to deserve this?

It's perplexing, you have caused a lot of trouble and dug a hole for yourself.

Just for a bit of extra money, you sold everything, leaving no memento for us.

What happened to his gallantry and campaign medals, and the family birth certificates?"

At no time did she make any effort to enter the house, kept just one foot on the step with the other firmly planted on the ground. Propriety was the last thing on her mind. She rattled her sentiments at Martin in the hope of preventing the situation from overwhelming her before having her complete say:

"There is more to life than just self-interest and money.

You have a duty to your family and others around you.

The way you treated the other German girl was bad enough but to grab everything and put the dog down, a dog father loved. It did not matter that it was getting old. It deserved better. We all deserved better.

Your desire for money is no excuse as you have a well-paid job and a wife that also works.

It is not good enough to justify your actions by just saying we all could have done it.

Just because you can does not justify it.

It is only about the rush for cash to join the loads of money brigade no matter what.

It is pure greed.

Well, have it your own way but do not expect any help from anyone else.

There are people with no humanity in them, but you were not brought up that way."

Throughout the scolding, Martin stood devoid of emotion. Betty's last act was the demand of all the family records followed by a silent show of strength to firmly indicate that she was not moving until this command was met. With the family photo album and birth certificates under her arm, she turned her back on the old family home and left, vanishing into the shadows. Tears ran down her cheeks as a tidal wave from the full force of grief from the death of her father and disbelief in the behaviour of her brother hit her.

Martin remained recalcitrant, never ever referred to his siblings or displayed any mementos of his family. No vindication for the house acquisition was offered to his friends who thought the property should have been shared with other family members. Despite this opinion, they shied away from direct criticism. In fact, after being initially surprised, Jason and the northerners quickly became indifferent to the land grabbing. The ex-council house was in a sought after area near a branch line railway station to up town. It required modernisation but was always going to bring a good yield; it was a banker.

As life settled down again, renovating the house and work ate up most of the time. Socialising was restricted to a few hours in the pub or lunch at home. The flat was sold as it made more sense to live closer to where Martin worked and use the profits on the house. They planned to turn the house into a desirable residence. It required a thorough going over as the interior had seen better days. The state of the wallpaper, the gathered dust and the grim odours of old man and dog hinted at a story of decline. While the exterior remained untouched, walls would be knocked through and wood flooring laid. With the addition of a modern kitchen and a walk-in shower unit, the house would be ideal for a professional couple wanting to escape up town. One of the first improvements was to returf the back garden, as a modern family had no need to grow its own fruit or vegetables. Only a low maintenance area was required for relaxing in hot sunny days.

In the years to come, the couple would never go outside the environs of Railhead except once up town on a sightseeing day with holidaying German relatives. The beauty of the Black Forest and its idyllic vision was to remain unchallenged. It was as if this country was famous for nothing at all to offer the motorcyclist or German visitor. Never toured around the country, never went on the great bike rides, never saw the countryside, and never developed a liking for its culture. No cruising through the pine forests of Scotland or along its lochs and seashores, no roaming along the open quiet roads of Northumbria, no winding runs in the Yorkshire Dales or testing the bike over the fells of Cumbria. In the end, the bike was ditched and a hard to get beige metallic *Wrangler Sahara* jeep bought as a replacement. This was deemed a better method of transport for shopping and carting bulk goods to the house. It was also a visible expression of their new status as successful money earners.

Work and the desire to earn as much money as possible ultimately became an obsession for the couple. The world around them could have fallen into chaos and they would not have noticed. Martin knew he had to raise capital and just wanted to get on with it, to get it over with as quickly as possible to ensure that work was finished and done with. If that involved working all the hours, day or night, so be it. Giving up on holidays was seen as a minor inconvenience if it meant sooner liberation from labour. Intense repetitiveness in the coming years would just have to be suffered in silence. Life became nothing other than improving the bank balance, clinging to the hope of a good life to come rather than living one. Each month ticked off when the wage packet arrived.

Martin volunteered to be permanently on nightshift

and took all the overtime that was going. This attitude led to working twelve-hour shifts for three weeks at a time; effectively trebling his basic wage to become a blue-collar worker that earned more than his bank manager. However, there was a price to pay and that price was years of monotony. Two hours of sitting at a production line followed by a thirty-minute break sitting in an enormous, empty canteen became his way of life. Two hours of sitting in subdued light watching chemical emulsions being sprayed onto film while wearing a mask for protection followed by thirty minutes in artificial light to allow his pupils to rest.

At night, a crew of forty maintained the twenty-four-hour film-processing unit in a site that required a daytime staffing level of six hundred. The place became a ghost town with all unnecessary lighting, heating and manufacturing equipment switched off. Martin was cold-shouldered by many of the workers. Ostracised by crewmembers siding with his long-serving brother and disgusted at the ingratitude shown for his sibling's efforts to get him a position that many other workers would have given a right eye for. Only a few men remained completely indifferent to the family feud. As was life, the socialising chitchat skills of these people were minimal. They were either 'yes' men or nighthawks like him who accepted all the overtime that was going. However, unlike him, these co-workers had no dream of escape, this was their existence and in a perverse way was preferred: being outside and ignored by mainstream society allowed personal inhibitions or unsocial behaviours never to be exposed or opened to ridicule.

For Martin, alcohol and caffeine gradually became the means of getting through bad days, when the thought of repeating the same painfully dull tasks did overwhelm him. Apart from the money earned, there was no other pretext to justify his insistence on working all the hours possible. As a blue-collar worker, there was no false luxury of conning himself that he was progressing up the company ladder and that his contribution made a difference. The only reward that awaited him was seeing his bank balance grow.

The mission to obtain a better life never considered health risks. It was assumed that his body would cope and all it took was strong willpower to see the job done. His physiology would endure what was thrown at it. He was still young, strong and anyway it would only be for a few years. The combined effects of poor sleep, unnatural working conditions, long-term exposure to chemicals and prolonged periods of unsocial hours did not discourage him. Irregular biological rhythms became the norm, as the body clock could not use natural daylight and darkness to regulate itself. It too like everything else in the country became deregulated. Core functions followed suit as all of them took their cue from this internal regulator. The cardiovascular, metabolic, digestion and immune systems along with hormonal balance had to sink or swim.

In terms of lifestyle, working odd hours led to some other understandable problems. During the long periods of night work, cut off from friends and the interests that gave him pleasure, his social life suffered; all key necessities for maintaining a good mood. What's more, he hardly exercised, rarely walked, always drove, became one of those people that thought it was crazy to walk, and was prone to eat junk food out of a handy vending machine at work or getting a takeaway or a pub meal when away from it. Blurred eyed and restless, it became habitual to drink a couple of cans of strong lager in the early mornings to help induce sleep during the day.

Martin and his wife rarely had time for intimate contact and bonding activities necessary to sustain a good relationship, only united couple one week out of the four and then shared activities mainly involved shopping and decorating the house. His days off work actually began to disrupt his wife's own established routine. She had her own job and house to run. The arrival of a lodger to help save money gave her a daily social contact. Better still, it was a female compatriot she got on with from the English language class for foreign residents she had attended which permitted shared interests and experiences to be articulated. This girl had come across to the South East to improve her already wonderfully spoken English by performing the duties of a living in *au pair*, however, she soon lost interest in this low paid constricted life, and was happy to escape it to spend her days lounging about the house when not doing casual bar work.

For the first time in living memory, Martin had to

visit the doctor when struck with a perpetual cold and other minor complaints. The doctor was old school and patiently listened to ascertain the patient's background. His diagnosis was not welcoming news. Sitting for days caused a niggling backache, which Martin's doctor diagnosed with the signs of nausea, heartburn and stomach problems as being psychosomatic due to the nature of his job, complicated by higher than expected blood pressure, blood sugar and cholesterol levels, and inevitably his gained weight. In strong words, it was clearly stated that he was taking his body for granted, and it was expressing its grievance and demand for amelioration to his daily regime. Any tinkling pain on the left-hand side was a warning not to be ignored. Another surprise was the need for prescription glasses more appropriate for an older man when he had only gone to an optician to get reactive lenses to help stop glare from sunlight from hurting his eyes, especially when driving home in the mornings. Deterioration in his central vision made it harder for him to read small print and importantly road signs. His body was giving up on him, like an ex-footballer, who was once a prime specimen, he found himself rushing into a premature middle age after only a few years of giving up on a healthy outdoor life.

Despite the warnings, something had cut off the use of his common sense as Martin kept this aggravating health news to himself and carried on regardless. The disregarded doctor's advice forced his body to take a different approach to make its complaint to be seriously taken by Martin. This time it opted for psychological warfare to dissuade him from continuing his relentless drive. *Our Leader* made its first appearance in the most unlikely setting. Martin was enjoying a quiet drink in a bar while his wife went shopping for her essentials. Freddi interrupted this calm moment when she returned, ordered a soft drink then commenced to relate her own workplace grievances to him. As she unloaded her built up tensions on to him, he held his head in his hands, wiped his weary eyes with his fingers as angst appeared on his face and his drink went flat. His spirit shrank with every concern expounded by his partner. The image of that scene from *Gone with the Wind* entered his mind when *Rhett Butler* told *Scarlett O'Hara* that he did not give a damn. As the undeterred Freddi rattled on, fatigue overtook him and transported him into a dream world of high politics:

On the pretext of insisting on someone who was forward thinking and not trapped in old mentality, Our Leader had just sacked an ageing MoD minister to install a younger dynamic rising star of the party. She had a reputation for filling the cabinet with young men, supposedly forever on the lookout for a suitable husband for her barmy daughter, so this decision was not seen as a shock. The chosen successor was a smug Martin, all scrubbed up and ready for the challenge ahead.

Sitting on a leather cushioned chair behind a large solid mahogany desk as the new appointee stood in front of her like an errant school boy waiting for his scolding, head bowed and hands behind his back,

Our Leader spelt out in a husky low voice what was expected of him. There was to be no screw-ups or talking to the press without her permission, and she demanded a personal briefing before any cabinet meeting to make sure she was always up to date on matters of state security.

Same room but different time, he finds himself once again alone with Our Leader. He had just finished that day's update. She informed him that she had kept an eye on him, was pleased with his progress and it was time he entered her inner sanctum. In future, he was to visit her in the evenings through a discrete entrance to No. 10. They could have a bite to eat while he performed his duties. All this was said in a promiscuous tone.

To Martin, the manner of this instruction sounded odd and uncalled for. So, knowing that she was on the lookout for a husband for her daughter, he felt honour bound to mention that he was in a long-term relationship and was not looking for a partner.

Fool cried out the angered woman:

'This had nothing to do with my daughter. I expect my ministers to be personally available 24/7.

Being Prime Minister is a full-time job and I demand that my ministers do what I say.'

'Sorry I thought you implied something improper,' uttered the profoundly apologetic Martin.

She stood up, ripped open her blouse and disclosed

her true intentions:

'Do not apologise. Underneath this PR created persona of a cold-hearted woman with not a slew of compassion, beats a heart that requires love. Am I not nubile and sexually alluring? Does power not make me attractive? Being married to an old man, I need someone on the side. You must obey me. Do as I demand. I am your leader.'

The astonished defence minister could only stare at her bare ample bosom.

'She does, she does have massive tits!'

"Are you listening to me," exclaimed Freddi.

Martin shuddered out of his fantasy to find Freddi looking quizzically across at him.

"Wipe your chin. You have been slobbering."

The presence of the lodger did not help his rattled nerves either. The sight of her skimpy knickers drying alongside the more robust hardwearing ones of his wife was always a distraction when within the confines of the bathroom. She was a beauty, several years younger than his wife and from the north of the country. Her name was Cara; a babe with a sinuous body exquisitely formed that moved gracefully: a heartbreaker. Whereas Freddi could be described as buck some, this young woman had small perky tits and a marginally raised backside, perfect for her slim body. Her hair was long flowing light brown, which highlighted her thin proportioned face with a button nose in the middle of it. Her presence was light and reassuringly erotic with skin that conveyed the impression of always being unblemished even when menstruating. In conversation, she stood a few inches apart, close but not quite touching. The warmth of her body and breath wafted into the nostrils as your face reflected from her sparkling brown eyes. A temptress that vowed never to be dominated, she tormented boyfriends with jealousy by assembling them all in the same room. A perfect example of what German engineering could produce!

It was only natural that everyone fancied her. Plain girls were easy prey and pretty ones were predators whereas Cara created mayhem everywhere she went. She was the embodiment of an enigmatic German film star, unconcerned of being what she was: full of vitality. Just playfully rubbing a man's lower back sent him into ecstasy. The most beautiful woman in the world and she rented a room in his house. Martin's eyes would light up when she came out of the bathroom after her shower with just a towel wrapped round her middle. The scent of her wet hair drove him crazy. After those freshly moisturised fine legs, smooth shoulders and slim arms disappeared into her bedroom, he would stare at the wet footprints, mesmerized until these evanescent works of beauty evaporated. The thought of the warm water that had just run down her back and between the clefts of her perfect cheeks stirred within his mind, mingled with some conflicting muses:

"Did Freddi invite her into the house to test my faithfulness?'

"Is it a reward for the hard work I have done?"

Cara gave him fever.

He regularly fantasised that Cara pressed herself against him, her scent overpowered him as she cupped her hands around his face and brushed her delicate palms smoothly down his cheeks, again only fantasising, submitted to all her desires. It was amazing how often they bumped into each other in the late mornings. On one occasion, his hand stretched out to squeeze her right cheek as she skipped out onto the landing with a cheerful acknowledgement that her ablutions were finished and the bathroom was free, but it froze when thoughts of negative repercussions flooded him.

Our Leader had to cry out even louder and be extremer in her demands for satisfaction to push fantasies involving the lodger into the background. This led to bizarre daydreams of *Our Leader* such as appearing as a scantily dressed dominatrix ready to punish her wicked little boy for his transgressions or in a threesome with her daughter and even ones with the old grey-haired husband looking on. The rich fullness of her breasts got more impressive the more triumphant and demanding she became, as if, like *page three girls*, she had resorted to artificial enhancements.

While Martin was experiencing daily conflicts

between reality and uncontrolled hallucinations fed by his rebelling subconscious, Freddi's understanding of the English language, its nuances and regional variations were progressing at a fair rate of knots.

On a fiercely hot Sunday afternoon in the South, as the rest of the country sat under a cloud covered sky, the couple and friends sat outside in the back garden. The squinting men huddled together at a table under an awning to avoid direct sunlight, accompanied by wasps circling the poured drinks as the women enjoyed the heat. On this occasion, Freddi expressed her surprise on hearing a work colleague state that the locals of Railhead did not have an accent. The comment came about when she mentioned that the northern accents sounded warmer and less sharp than theirs.

"They don't have accents here. The southerners believe they speak proper English," explained a northerner.

"But it does not sound like the English spoken on the *BBC*."

"It doesn't but they think it does! In fact, Cara speaks better posh English than anyone down here."

"I know she even speaks posh German!"

Cara looked up from her sunbathing and smiled. She was still musing over something one of the northerners had said when teasing her by suggesting that the gulf stream ran up the west coast along some of the best white sand beaches in the world. Did they think she was born yesterday? Why did men think pretty women were stupid or was it just a defence mechanism to delude themselves that the female of the species could not have brains and beauty.

With German savantism wrapped around her, the hostess's observations of daily life raised some interesting debates. One was the endless discussion about the roads and pavements being continually dug up. The smell of gas was still everywhere and travelling on foot or car was a hazardous exercise.

"Instead of re-digging up pavements why not lay out removable grills to allow access to boxed communications. It would be cheaper in the long run and nicer to the eye."

Everyone laughed at this suggestion and tried to explain that long-term planning was not the English way of doing things. Do it on the cheap today and leave it for someone else to pick up the cost of a necessary proper overhaul later on.

"Why does everything cost twice as much here?"

"Apparently, we like to pay premium prices for our goods as it raises our self-esteem," clarified a northerner.

"It does not matter anyway as it can all be put on the credit card, so it is not as if it is real money," chipped in Jason.

"Why don't deliverymen take old appliances away with them? There must be room in the van as they have just delivered a replacement. It is very silly."

To move the subject away from English bashing, Jason pointed out that the *hijab* had been spotted in Railhead and that the Bangladeshi community had been given permission to build a mosque on the site of an old courthouse. After an awkward silence, an unexpected ally was found in the form of the next-door neighbour, who volunteered his opinion from over the fence. An Indian, a father of two teenage daughters whose wife had a habit of making too much samosa and pakora that she gave to the young couple, augmented Jason's fears by declaring that the Muslims fucked up India and the same would happen here. This freely offered opinion was whole-hearted expressed while his eyes naturally focused on the stretched-out Cara, lying on a blanket with a book in her face and ankles wriggling away in the air, her body sizzling in the baking hot sun; her youthful hue the most perfect ornament for any garden. After the neighbour walked away, a northerner ventured to bait Jason:

"You are becoming a bigot?"

"Not really, I dispraise all religions and backward practices, we spent hundreds of years to turn them into an irrelevance and now outsiders want to make them mainstream again. I could easily say you guys are hypocrites. You complain about the dumbing down of society and the destruction of our language by inane sports presenters and crap TV but happily

profess to tolerate the influx of cultures that weaken
our society."

Martin smiled when memories of schooldays came
back to him.

To prevent the conversation from descending into
political nonsense, Freddi herded everyone indoors
to get ready for lunch. Martin showed the visitors
his latest acquisition. Perched at the top front corner
of the enlarged front room a small elegant raptor
looked down on them: a pretty small blue-grey and
brown hobby all the way from Germany; stuffed and
fitted with glass eyes that gave off the illusion of
glistening tears. During lunch, a northerner made a
faux pas when he let out that he had driven only two
makes of car, *VW* and *Nissan,* preferring the latter
manufacturer for the smoothness and turning
control of the Nippon vehicles. This revelation
resulted in a smaller dessert portion, however, Cara
made up for the frost in international relations by
rubbing his back. Over coffee, to make amends the
same northerner pointed out how practical German
biscuits were compared to UK manufactured ones.
In between munching an example of one, his
reasoning was explained:

"You have the chocolate inside the biscuit, not on the
outside, so no messy fingers."

More drinks followed the soul enhancing meal as
R.E.M played out of wall-mounted speakers. The

men turned down the proposal to play card or board games and rejected out of hand Freddi's attempt to get her pop greatest hits cd played. They had found their tongues and had no intention of changing the train of thought or having their ears polluted. The women vanished for a short period to let the men talk rubbish. Freddi tidied up in the kitchen as Cara watched. The lodger was dissuaded from helping about the house after her adoption of the cunning male tactic of doing more damage than good. Later, the utterly relaxed and transparent straight talking Freddi unwind with a glass of hock, a cigarette and talked about her own favourite subject, the antics of Jason; her guilty pleasure:

"No passionate parts in him. Does not have natural feelings and is too wrapped up in himself.

Who would want to marry him? Women expect to be looked after, not the other way round.

How can he get credit cards, when he never works? He shirks any activity not involving beer.

How can he live this way?"

Elated by the attention, a magnanimous Jason just uttered a snigger, nodded in her direction, and with the same gesture used to turn down the chance to eat a home-cooked meal, a hand was waved in the air in ironic acknowledgement of her comments before standing up to get another drink. A long silence developed as all eyes were on Jason, waiting for his inevitable wisecrack. The butt of his lighted cigarette was stubbed out in the shared ashtray by pressing and twisting it until extinguished. Once he had obtained an appropriate lull in the conversation, Jason chimed:

"You can laugh all you want, but I have to have things my own way.

It is the age of equality so men can just be as frivolous and self-absorbed as women. If a woman wanted to be the breadwinner, I would not complain. Surely a true sign of female liberation is being willing to look after us men."

Stating the obvious, Freddi without any hint of malice countered:

"The women aren't exactly beating a path to your door to take that role on."

Everyone laughed.

Raising his glass in the air, Jason faked a grin, a broad one, to his audience.

Freddi flashed him a feigned smile in return.

It was true that Jason no longer gave the impression of finding an occupation that would interest him or even allow him to make use of his wits; to turn ideas into literature or even get a job in journalism, an honoured profession where his rich vocabulary could easy be employed to insinuate evil doings in anyone with no reporting of any goodness found in that person, only embellished muck. The same conclusion of all loafers had been reached that somebody else would solve his and the world's problems. One of the northerners could be his *Boswell*. It would save him the effort of having to write down his great social observations.

"My role in life is to regale the masses of my imitable wit," declared the tipsy Jason, as he once again topped up his glass with lager and helped himself to one of Freddi's cigarettes, and lighted it with her throwaway lighter that rested on the top of the unbranded packet. The health lobby ongoing debate about banning tobacco advertising seemed impervious to the fact that many smokers bought unbranded cigarettes for the price and fact that the taste was not much different from the more expensive advertised options.

With a perspicuous insight of youth while munching some *matchmakers*, Cara retorted in support of the sisterhood:

"Self-obsession in men not only tortures them, it is a red warning flag to women to leave them well alone."

As the two insurmountable forces continued their polemic deliberations, the rest of the party sat back, relaxed, and without listening very hard, enjoyed the show that always ended with no clear winner. The protagonists had something in common after all; both spoke their unwavering minds.

The evening's conversations were not all centred

around Jason. Cara managed to talk about matters that were more important; she was excited because she had recognised a film star in the village video shop: it was *Tom Cruise.* He had smiled at her. It was another sign of the improved status of the district. Instead of being an enclave of a working-class past, the place had turned into a desirable area for the *nouveau riche.* The roll of shops on the road to up town had been relabelled as a village by the estate agents and was happily adopted by the neighbourhood. Film stars with the latest love interest, in between filming at studios and spending the evenings in rented nearby mansions, were often reported to be seen in the village. Not only did it have a video shop but also delis and a wine importer had recently moved in. It furthermore became commonplace for the faces of footballers and media created celebs to be spotted driving past or posing in the many refurbished bars.

On the way home, the lads had a final few drinks in one of their favourite pubs. Jason, as usual, avoided buying the early rounds in case the session turned into a binge and had to pay his way; the day Jason voluntarily bought the first round of drinks would be a day to remember. Sitting around the accustomed table with the smoke rising from the ashtray directed away from the habitual smokers among them, the men reflected on Freddi's unflinching national pride. Jason found her unsophisticated directness amusing and suggested that it was best to take no notice and just patronise her while the northerners thought Martin should make the effort to broaden her horizons:

"A closed mind has to be opened?"

"How can Freddi develop a real understanding of the country if she does not visit anywhere. Martin should take her round the country."

Sighing and shaking his head, Jason somewhat haughtily dismissed these observations. In a rare moment of sympathetic feeling for others or maybe to just to be argumentative, he defended the couple's life choices:

"Nonsense. It is useless to concern yourself about how other people wished to spend their lives. Let people live their own way. Why do liberals have a mania for wanting everyone to be like them?

You should not insinuate that their existence is full of folly or even pointless. They are only looking after themselves.

Their simple aspirations and lack of metaphysical thought make life an easier and happier experience."

As Jason spoke up for the defence of hardworking friends, an illuminated detail from the large panoramic medieval scene on the wall behind him, showed a not so cunning delighted rascal pilfering apples from a barrel being filled by tired looking peasants.

In the meantime, Martin had invariably falling asleep on the couch. His body by this time had upped the ante as far as hallucinations were concerned. He was now experiencing an occurring delirious dream. It involved sirens dancing and whirling above him as he lay flat out on his back on driftwood as waves tossed and plummeted around him. The swirling temptresses came in and out of focus teasing him with promises of aid only to pull away at the last moment. Scantily dressed in see-through silks, the cries of seduction drove him wild. Faster and faster they spun, laughing and giggling with joy. Singing a chant about how men made war and women wanted love. Occasionally one would poke her face down close to his exhausted own, smirk and fleetingly kiss him. The faster the spinning the more vivid and bright the sensation became. The climax that woke him was always the same. The faces of Freddi, Cara and *Our Leader* would all glide down together and cry out:

"Which one, which one do you want?"

BACK TO EDEN

It was the epoch of anxiety stirring three-letter acronyms. Acronyms were not new and had been fermenting away in the brains of bureaucrats for years. However, inevitably, the usage of them spread across the land like invading alien plant and vermin species. Acronyms like *DNA, HIV, BSE* and *ERM* became every day speak, each of them conjuring up a possible cold and even threatening vision of the future.

Man had been decoded allowing the perfect baby to be produced by test-tube scientists with all generic weaknesses and irrational self-harming behaviours eliminated. Rich white gays fucking chimps in Africa had been blamed for the creation of an extinction-threatening virus. Meat-eaters in old age would turn into brain-dead zombies. Monetary policy depended on what foreign agents were doing. In other words, sex was not only an emblem of power but from now also one of death as predators ruthlessly left a modern killer behind with their seeds; while herbivores were forced to become cannibals to satisfy the demand from powerful supermarkets for cheap manufactured meat; and a duplicitous anti-European campaigning government manipulated interest rates for years to allow them to follow rates set in the European Union, rates bolstered by the strength of a German powerhouse economy. All because it was a matter of pride to demonstrate that a financial sector led economy fuelled by customer spending could take on traditional industrial might.

Bovine Spongiform Encephalopathy had been bubbling away quietly for several years. Warnings about it being unnatural for animals to eat themselves went unheeded. Man had apparently discovered how to extract protein without leaving any hint of the original source. Once admitted, the diseased meat was dismissed as not harmful to humans. Later, it was then decided to confess there was a slight possibility of harm. The good news, it only affected the poor cuts, so in the words of the Prime Minister, there was nothing for the party's voters to worry about. Her farming minister with granddaughter in toll was duly put in front of the press to be seen eating quality cuts of minced beef burger meat. Unfortunately, a human variant, *Creutzfeldt–Jakob disease* (another three-letter acronym), caused the deaths of several hundred people and completely wiped out the confidence of anyone on the planet in eating British beef. *Les rosbifs* were in disgrace. Four hundred thousand dead cattle and countless slaughtered sheep later, at the cost of billions, people still mistrusted the food industry. Along with spending on cures for *HIV* and compensation for contaminated insulin products, billions of taxpayers' money had to be diverted into activities to avert man-made disasters caused by hubristic, sexual and financial greediness. Money and skills that would have saved more lives if spent on less politically emotive research.

Over in America, the financial guru having had instructed his agents to support the government now commanded them to use the international money market to bring it down. For several months, his financial house had bought up a huge position in sterling. It was time to make capital out of a crash, create billions for his investors and more importantly for himself. The repercussions would be felt all across the land. This wealth creator and his clients made a fortune from the rapid deregulation of the country and now would make another fortune by bringing the economy down, causing mortgage repayment misery and loss of jobs.

The command was sent out to sell sterling. *Black Wednesday* terrified a nation, temporarily humbled politicians, and thrilled economical experts debating among themselves all the possible outcomes for a nation completely dependent on the financial sector for its wealth. At the end of the day, the pound withdrew from the *European Exchange Rate Mechanism*. Speculators by short selling sterling made billions of pounds in profit on this notorious

day. The pound had to be devalued with the
government losing tens of billions in its failed
attempt to prop it up. With interest rates at 15%
and inflation three times that of Germany, boom
went to bust. The good days were over. Small
businesses failed and international companies
decided to move out of the country. The press barons
in attempting to support the government failed to
diffuse the enormity of the collapse. Only the banks
were safe, protected in fortress towers of concrete
and steel, buffered by Arab black gold. As the
politicians ran about apportioning blame on others,
the banks kept the nation afloat.

Railhead suffered badly. Overnight it became a sad
dark place, a town with malice. Even the wild birds
suddenly insinuated a sinister dark side and became
argumentative with each other. The murmuration of
starlings, the tidings of magpies and increased
flocks of feral pigeons all became noisy and
mischievous, swooping down to fight over human
refuse. The human population mirrored the
behaviour of these feathered creatures. Anger and
dread manifested themselves as people looked for
scapegoats to their problems. People trundled about
with heads down, permanently on edge. Fights
broke out over scratches on inanimate objects,
arguments erupted at queues as barging and ill
manners became prevalent, shoppers demanded
better and instant service while car horns blasted
away for the least delay. Social respect was
dismissed as archaic nonsense; it was as if *Essex* had
expanded overnight to cover the whole of the Home
Counties. Promiscuous young females and males sat

in beer gardens loudly deliberating whether they would shag a new young celebrity or sports star as children played around them. The constant media coverage of mad cow disease and *HIV* did not help quell heightened nerves. It tainted the taste of everything that was eaten and worried parents concerned about what the authorities were putting in the school meals.

The Prime Minister had gone loopy: rumoured to have been sneakily fed dodgy meat by disgruntled Westminster restaurant staff, she subsequently managed to get herself mauled by a sheep, carted away by men in grey suits, and locked up on the top floor of an Arab owned luxury hotel with the key thrown away. Last heard screaming that the Palace should always inform her what the queen will be wearing that day.

All talk of being able to buy castles up north ceased. The air felt cold again as people despaired for the future, especially the newly mortgaged not accustomed to large debt. Fraud was ripe, causing massive increases in house and car insurance payments. Customers denied receiving parcels in the post, repair shops and car mechanics contrived higher bills to defraud insurance companies and TV aerial installations were claimed under storm damage claims. Disability levels substantially jumped helped by the spiralling in the number of car accidents that resulted in impossible to disprove backlash injuries. Town centre streets became jammed packed with cars displaying disabled stickers. It was as if, a war had been declared and not reported by the media under *section D.*

In good times, women were fussy, choosy creatures with the only men capable of getting their attention being the acceptable good-looking braggers promising to deliver. Now in these hard economic times, others with safe jobs had a chance to pull them. They became the modern equivalent of the conquering soldiers with bars of chocolate and nylons in their rucksacks.

For Martin and his friends, the seediness that pervaded Railhead made the biggest impact. Depravity was literally in the faces of drinkers in all the clubs and bars, as owners were offered cheap sleazy entertainment to lure customers. Knocking shops and pubs lock-ins were thriving businesses. One pub became notorious for having gartered female bar staff who provided all types of extras after hours. Another pub continuously showed porn movies on its big screen, clearly visible from the street. Like most things in the country, it was an unregulated market only requiring willing or financially stricken volunteers to offer their goods. These were not shipped in foreigners but mainly local women of all ages making a few pounds by degrading themselves. An early evening drink could be interrupted by a half-starved naked girl displaying her wares while a smartly dressed fuller figured female boss come minder watched by the side of the bar. The beer spoilt by having a bruised looking anus thrust into the face. The danseuse either had a bad case of diarrhoea or she had other duties to perform that involved penetrating her rear with hard instruments. The pleasure of a late midweek evening drink spoilt by the antics of the next table whose idea of fun was calling up a stripagram agency to hire an old granny in a revealing short wedding dress outfit to appear and perform her act. The game old bird mishandled by each young man as they forced her to sit on their laps. Her bare breasts rubbed while photos were taken. Walking home at night had new problems, apart from the mugging, there was the likelihood of being accosted in badly lit streets by women inviting you back to their house, some acting as madams for daughters.

"Want a good time?"

Like in all free markets, the quality on offer varied with some of these new entrepreneurs being class acts that could look after themselves. One, in particular, came from up town once a week to entertain a pub packed with building site workers; a blond stripper, a strong nubile healthy beast probably in her mid-twenties but looked older due to her challenging vocation. Worldlier wise than one of the northerners she looked out for to entrust with her gear as she stripped and danced while skilfully navigating the tight spaces between tables, chairs and bulky guys bringing drinks from the bar, all the time ignoring any crude call and brushing off wandering hands in the audience. How the northerner got this job as guardian of the clothes was a mystery, but every week she expected him to be there on hand to help:

"It is so sweet of you."

A true professional, an enlisted clothes guardian
was probably in every pub visited; pubs she never
left until everyone who heckled or tried to touch her
arse or boobs had put money into the passed round
plate. Her plate always ran over, making the weekly
journey to Railhead worthwhile.

If Martin was in the company then drink sessions
continued to end with him outside at the corner of a
street, flat on his back, sprawled out, feet and arms
waving, staring up at the stars and appearing to be
engrossed in conversation with invisible phantoms,
his own pink elephant creations. Occasionally kicked
and shoved by his companions to keep the flapping
friend under some sort of control as they waited for
the cavalry to arrive. The last thing Martin half
remembered on those occasions was being hauled up
the stairs by his wife; his arm around her neck while
she cursed how heavy her husband had become. For
Freddi, it gave rise to a listless night's sleep as her
husband tossed and turned, mumbling in his sleep
about national defence issues and standing his man
to attention when given some unheard command.

For months, it was apparent to all that Martin was
visibly putting on more weight and increasingly
susceptible to slumping over after just a few pints.
However, such concerns took a back seat as life once
again turned out good for him. Recessions had
winners and losers, and another bit of good fortune
was on the way to him, he was to be made
redundant, not a get out of this door immediately

redundancy, but a controlled one agreed by the union resulting in a lucrative deal. The global enterprise that employed him wanted to relocate this part of its business to Germany, returning machinery to where it was manufactured. It wanted to do this with the minimum of fuss and disruption to its business. Subsequently, key workers on the twenty-hour production line were handsomely rewarded for their continued goodwill and placidity. At the same time, the house had not lost much value due to its excellent state of repair and prime location. With accumulated savings, the disposal of the house and fittings, along with final pay packets, the couple had amassed a fortune, they were near the touchline to fulfil the goal of the hard work and single-mindedness that had driven them for years. A sum that should be sufficient to allow them to build a home in the Black Forest.

Around seven years after arriving back penniless, an incredible alleviation in Martin's financial situation had occurred in these intervening years, he would be returning to Germany, a much richer man. All required possessions, lock, stock and barrel, were gathered up, put in a six-wheeled freight carrier and transferred to Germany with the happy couple following in the jeep. Like spawning salmon, the way back was known by heart. They would travel to *Dover*, get the ferry to *Calais*, and cut across northeast France via *Lens, Reims* and *Metz* to *Strasburg* then south to the border and the Black Forest. All the time keeping to the national road routes, stopping only at service stations. Their quest for a better life was almost over.

Although they did not expect to miss Railhead, Jason would be missed. The good-byes were emotional, involving strong handshakes and hugs, and plenty of drink on the lead up to the actual leaving day. Cara had already moved on and was in Germany finding herself a wealthy husband. On the day of departure, Freddi was touched by Jason's long face. However, the displayed disconsolation was not just fuelled by his friends' leaving but also by the banks' refusals to extend his credit limits. His custom was no longer sought after; society had turned its back on him, leaving him desolate and angry, cruelly left in penury; a junkie denied a fix by his suppliers.

Euphoria had set in and the couple only saw good, happy times ahead. Once established, friends would always be welcomed anytime in Germany. The homeward bound couple should be easy to find in *Brettengen*:

"It will be the big house on the summit of the hill!"

On the day of departure, friends scraped their heels as the convoy headed away accompanied by music from the jeep's tape deck. When *'Bat Out Of Hell'* had faded away, all trotted off to a nearby pub to raise a toast to the already missed migrants.

****

The couple knew late on that an immediate return to the village was not possible. There was nothing available to house all their wares. There was no land on the market to purchase either. They had been misinformed about a property that would be available when finalising plans to move, so in the meantime, they would have to bide time until something appropriate came on the market. This resulted in them moving to a nearby town that had sufficient rented accommodation. This was Sunny *Freiburg*, a fairy tale setting full of history and culture, with plenty of good eateries. Located near the Swiss border with views of distant snow-capped mountains, a scenic medieval town built on southern foothills, surrounded by vineyards, very alpine in appearance and only a few miles from a busy regional airport on the Swiss side of the border. Not a bad place to hang out, relax and wait for a permanent place to live. The rented accommodation was a large flat in an apartment block inhabited by people with a good socioeconomic status.

The happy couple got off to a good start. The different milieu revamped their marriage. Eager to please, none could do no wrong. Instead of keeping the bed warm for each other as one went to bed and the other left it, there was the sharing of warmth and pillow talk, not quite drowning in each other's eyes like young lovers but close enough as increased endorphin levels rejuvenated their gaits. They walked about with all the senses invigorated, holding hands, strolling round ornate streets, side by side, matching strides, touching, linking arms, Freddi unconsciously waving her head and smiling as her husband walked in a virile manner, both taking shared pleasure in what was seen.

Decent coffee was enjoyed whiling sitting outside in a market square or next to a calm flowing canal. Appreciating how the local municipality managed to provide up to date communications and a good transport system while keeping its cobbled roads and pavements in an original state.

They acclimatised to the distinct German sounds around them; picking out idiosyncrasies that told them which region the owner of voice came from. His wife laughing at any terrible guess from Martin, who was still trying to retune his hears. In this border town of many nationalities, the only way to distinguish the origins of people was by language. The colour of the skin, dress sense and mannerism never an apparent giveaway unless the person was a stereotypical caricature dreamed up by a tourist marketing board. Mundane activities became interesting. Freddi enjoyed buying and preparing meals with fresh, familiar and much-missed ingredients. The cost of living was compared with prices paid in England. Politeness was expressed with vigour as *'danke vielmals'* filled the air. The joy of seeing a distant horizon bathed in sunlight hills was edifying after years of seeing nothing beyond the end of a street. Never disappointed, everything smelt fresh, excellent food was aplenty and frothing cellar-cooled beer was available to drink.

They did the inevitable tour of all the local relatives and retold their plans to everyone. At a friend's house, everyone laughed with Martin when he pointed out that a five-year-old daughter of an old biker chum, an attractive young blond haired girl, was going to grow up to be a heartbreaker. As the men drank beer and listened to *Guns and Roses* in the lounge with Martin explaining some of the hard to translate lyrics, the women chatted as they tidied up in the kitchen. It had been a long time since Freddi had a girly chat in her own tongue with a glass of wine in her hand:

"Aren't you going to start a family Freddi?"

"Of course, I have actually stopped taking the pill since we have been back. It will be a good surprise for Martin. The sex has been better as well. I am sure he has grown another couple of centimetres!"

"Why have you waited so long?"

"I want a German baby."

They both smiled and hoped that the stork would not be late.

On the downside, catching up on how everyone had fared over the last few years, revealed tales of breakups and misfortune. The arrival of the free to travel East Germans had swelled the labour market making good earnings more difficult to find. Some old friends, like Gunnar, had moved away to get work up north. Others still had normal busy outdoor lives with the addition of children to become typical time and cash short families, surviving one unexpected crisis to the next. All complained about the abundance of empty second homes due to the influx of rich northern outsiders with cash to splash.

Christmas in the Black Forest rekindled their love affair with the scenery and its traditions. Soaking up the festival atmosphere at open-air markets, as fires blazed sending the smell of roasting meat into the crisp night air to mingle with sweet herbs and cinnamon emanating from the bakers' stalls. The predictable dry cold of the continent felt refreshing after years of damp uninspiring insipid winters in Railhead. German vocalists excelled themselves at this time of year with an array of instantly recognisable holiday songs; after all, this region invented the traditional Christmas. The couple munched Christmas cookies and sampled the many flavours of schnapps when visiting relatives. Happy to watch *Dinner For One* for the hundredth time as every TV channel broadcasted it. Winter walks wearing bright warm clothes, skiing and snowboarding all within easy reach while dipping wholesome pieces of bread into melted cheese made more sense when snow fell outside. It may have been cold outside but they kept each other's heart warm.

As should have been expected, life rarely ran smoothly for long and the wait in *Freiburg* turned into months. Plenty of sympathy was still being offered for the difficulty in securing a place in the village when competing against *Frankfurt* executives and the likes, but, little nuisances started to surface as the clean, bright apartment block on the outskirts of town started to reveal the true nature of modern living for town dwellers. On the outside and to the new arrival the cream coloured seven-storey building with private balconies within a manicured green setting looked appealing. The neighbours were friendly and polite when met in elevators or hallways. Car parking was conveniently placed in the basement and the rear of the building. Nonetheless, the apartment was a glorified homogeneous unit, a place for careerists and work addicts to rest at night when prime activities had been completed. An open prison waiting for the day releases to return before curfew.

Small things became apparent over time. They effectively lived in a featureless straight edged box with only functionality and rational thought behind its design. Each unit resembled the other: twenty-eight units per block; eight concrete blocks in the green field estate; all with identical built-in appliances. The manifestation of unexpected noise above their heads surprised a couple used to living in a purpose-built family home. The block was a microcosm of personas with the majority of residents wishing to be anonymous, a few instinctively openly friendly and the remainder indifferent verging on rudeness. Outside, the block, there was nothing to do within walking distance. Nor were they culture vultures nor sports enthusiasts that could take full advantage of the historic surrounds and first-rate equipped sports centres.

Life in Germany slowly commenced to not match Martin's expectations. Integration into a new environment proved difficult for the non-working Martin. The time rich, TV averse man became isolated and without a purpose because he had nothing meaningful to do. DIY was out of the

question as the concierge was the only one licenced
to conduct maintenance and small repair work in
the apartments. He lacked a good general interest to
get him out of the flat to whittle away the abundant
free time, unlike his wife accustomed to performing
daily activities and completely relaxed about doing
small chores. Meeting other like-minded social
drinkers proved difficult to find as he lacked local
knowledge for easy chitchat. The presence of friends
who were always available for relaxed, easy
company was badly missed.

The Jasons of this world did have a role to play.

Early attempts at producing the wanted heir were
fruitless; and later, lovemaking became less
enjoyable and more formulated to maximise the
chances of successful impregnation. Alterations were
made to their daily intake with the two of them
agreeing to eschew caffeine and significantly cut
down alcohol consumption. These abstinences were
easier to bear for the woman than the man. Going
cold turkey with the accompanied withdrawal pains
increased Martin's stress levels causing him to
resort to painkillers to alleviate the pressure. He
experienced periodic sharp pain up the side of his
neck and anxiety flushes as he felt his blood
pressure rise. It was a reminder that he enjoyed
these stimulants and that his body craved them.
Never a day passed without the demand from an
inner voice for an about-turn:

"I want a drink."

"It is unnatural to not partake in a refreshing drink."

"As unnatural as seeing an albino playing the saxophone in a jazz band."

"Just one."

Many months passed and still no baby came. Lack of providence and no deep understanding of the role power politics played in a relationship now led to unforeseen shifts in the circumstances of the couple. Their relationship began to sunder as they got jaded being joined at the hip with previous unspoken tensions and frictions seeing daylight. A partnership that was so strong and that had held together despite many difficult situations in England started to show cracks. It appeared that too much time cooped up together had weakened their bond. Sex became a chore. Martin tried hard to remain erect by fantasising about the old lodger Cara and returning the lesbian female warrior *Xena* back to the fold. This did temporarily aid his efforts but the bizarre image of *Our Leader* suddenly appearing in his mind quickly deflated him. The endeavours of the past decade became tainted by the unfulfillment of the dream.

A check-up with the doctor had declared that Freddi was capable of children. The summer, they first met, she was in her early twenties, a time when everything was straightforward and easy, sleeping together with a combination of frivolity and lust. It started a chain of events that had eventually led to the present day. She was now over thirty and had doubts. Continually working in unsocial conditions at the prime of his life had weakened her husband, made him soft, unfit, prone to chronic illness, physically old before his time, and he was probably incapable of producing healthy sperm.

Attempts of upping his sperm count by the use of vitamins and the right nutrition proved useless. *O mice and men* taught at school now made sense to Martin.

Unexpected consequences raised their ugly heads. Freddi created independent roots when she got a job that got her out of the house. Something, which allowed her, to feed her own addiction to have something useful to do. She had glanced an advert for a position similar to her last job in England, except this local company dealt with all the countries around it, using English as the business language. It was foolish not to apply for it. The money would stop them eating too deeply into hard earned savings. At the interview, her keenness, openness and several years of experience in an English working environment, made her a shoe-in. Martin misread this action as a declaration of her intent to give up on the idea of children.

He spent a lot of time sitting and gazing with his mind filled with a deflated nothingness that sometimes permeated people who had spent a long time focused on achieving a goal at the detriment of all else only to find the result had not made the impact that was expected. He recognised the sound of every creaking floorboard in the flat. He learnt some interesting new facts: snails travelled nippily when not watched and plants like kids grew in spurts. It occurred to him that it took great inner strength to be able to do nothing, just ponder about life and not let unsettling thoughts upset you. Otherwise, he was bored shitless, had resumed drinking and kept swallowing the painkillers he had substituted it for. The cuckoo clock in the lounge struck the hour in an unloved rented apartment.

The biggest revelation for Martin was the realisation that he could not regain the energy and strength of old and was now sedentary and reluctant to enter the job market again. He had no German qualifications or certificates of competence to show employers if he applied for anything above the role of a labourer. Labouring was ok when young but not after years of sitting at a production line waiting for a mechanical mishap to happen. The old Germany he loved was vibrant and exciting because he was young. Everything seemed special when life was opening up in front of you. Youth coloured your vision to skew your observations. It was impossible to truly envisage being stuck in a rut when many options were in easy reach. However, behind the rosy glow, life was always more complex, dark and a long hard fight to maintain one's place in the world.

Life was just as mundane here as it could have been in Railhead. At the appointed hour with German precision, doors flipped open; a mechanical wheel turned then the expectant sound radiated out:

"Cuc-koo, Cuc-koo..."

The alert from the cuckoo clock took on sinister undertones. It was no longer a friendly emission of sound to inform the residents of the time. It was a cry for help, a plea to be rescued, to be freed from the nail that pinned it to the clock. The promised life had also been stolen from it.

In relationships, trials never ended. Good times and unhappiness followed each other like night and day. Only the continued belief in the unsaid reason for being together allowed couples to persevere their sanity. The natural tensions that occurred between couples that knew each other inside out produced serious disruptive undercurrents. Points of no return in silly arguments become regular events. Time, as measured by Man, was chronological, but emotional skirmishes were circular in nature as arguing about the same ensuing issues created an unbreakable rut. Disputes were not rational problems but ones based on raw emotions that required someone to accept an altered stance to allow unhealthy tensions to disperse. However, common sense spoke too late or took a back seat when emotions flared. The desires that were not deemed necessary for daily physical health tended to be the ones that brought real pleasure or spiritual comfort. Irrational behaviour provoked estrangements that only heightened this irrationality, creating an endless feedback of negative energy that promised a traumatic climax. An inevitable crisis compounded by inadequacies to think of an agreed way to cope with any unwelcomed crisis.

One person was speeding along on a new route and the other determinedly stuck on the old path. This wife was not that different from the girl he married just older and seeking some independence. Aspirations evolved with age, circumstances and available opportunities. She was programmed to work to the end of her days. Of course, other unsaid reasons for the need to work may have come into it. The maturing woman may now not have liked the idea of staying with her partner but was reluctant to admit it. Her upbringing and learnt mores barred the idea of divorce. She did not have the understanding or mentality to grasp her husband's strange maudlin behaviour. To his wife, he was unrecognisable from the man she married. In her world, you pulled yourself together and got on with it. Melancholic people were not a mystery to be comprehended but dismissed. She stubbornly refused to scrutinise life, to explore any feelings of unease. The realisation that having children was unlikely did not upset her that much. She believed in doing the best that was possible under the circumstances so was content to continue working, make money. She could always indulge any motherly affection on her nieces and cousins.

Martin was still silently suffering from the symptoms of burn out after years of living a shallow life. Just being alive was not good enough; he could not let the dream of a better life fade away. Eating and beer drinking dominated his days. His sporadic back problems did not help his mood. Sitting on a chair, jaws tight, he would stare for hours, not into space but inward, pulled into a darkness that trapped his train of thought as life continued around him, moving on, changing. The deeper he went, the harder it was to come back. In his mind's eye, shutters closed down, heavy shutters that took a considerable amount of willpower to push up.

Freddi attempted to reassure her husband that there was nothing doing on, that the plan to start a family was still a priority, but in the interim, she enjoyed her job. In her new position, her role was shown in the office staff organisation chart as directly under the command of *Herr Direktor* while everyone else had to settle for being listed under various departments and teams. She loved looking at this chart. The less philosophical the person, the more likely he or she to adopt the stakeholder role!

At home, as frustrations rose, it came to the stage that she would walk about tight lipped with a permanent frown as a defence against any criticism of her engaging in the world of work when the rewards to earn the right to relax and enjoy the fruits of previous labours had already been gathered.

"So, we just continue to work as if that what life is about," moaned her husband.

She, in a slow manner like talking to a foreigner, told him to stop niggling her. In the end, the bedtime routine settled into a silent and uncomfortable affair. Lying together, she imaged that she could almost hear the same questions whirling in his head. Doubts and questioning that choke everything like a vine that wrapped itself around all other flora. There was no way back and a wave of despair struck her. Dissociation between the couple was firmly set. Both knew that the long-awaited confrontation was getting ever so closer. One day one of them would commit themselves to the final solution. At least the wife knew she was on home soil.

As time went by, Freddi gave her job the highest priority and staying late in the office to proof read letters that had to be dispatched that night became a regular occurrence. She happily threw herself into it, believed what she was doing mattered. Being essentially the PA to the top man, who after years of working his way up from the shop floor now depended on the efforts and successes of the staff. *Herr Direktor* was a small balding officious man that was determined to hold onto his well-paid position no matter what. Climbing the ladder taught him all the tricks of the trade and no one was going to pull the wool over his eyes and dethrone him. He had a wife and four greedy teenage daughters to feed so needed this job for a long time to come. All his girls had the same rotund barrel shape as him which gave him confidence that he was only feeding his own. Freddi became indispensable to him. *Herr Direktor's* English was poor and he began to rely heavily on Freddi to make sure he avoided costly misunderstandings. This gave her a confidence boost that nourished an ego that enjoyed being fed. She had her own little office with an adjoining door to his office. The boss's reliance on her meant she would not be allowed to do anything else, be kept in the same position, and not advance. Doing the same routine until made redundant or something catastrophic happened.

Once you get to know anyone, you find in their own unique way they are mad and self-deluded, but so long as people continued to give the illusion of functioning normally within society then acceptance was assured. In Martin's case, the barrier that kept private eccentricity hidden was breaking down. He was overwrought and obsessed about his wife's activities in and out of work. Paranoia was ripe. In a state of nervous tension fuelled by alcohol, his mind ran riot. Febrile questioning stayed with him, night and day. Breakups in marriages usually involved more than the couple. Her preoccupation with work never failed to baffle Martin to such an extent that he manifested alternative reasons for her devotion to it. The same questions without resolution lingered in Martin's mind; a mind full of flux that he no longer controlled. Was she having an office affair? Did she meet up again with an old boyfriend that she had accidentally run into? The possibility of an office affair was always at the top of the list of the recurring questions. He had to determine the truth.

Compulsion led to incipient madness through to complete visible breakdown. Paranoia was the destroyer of souls. Distorted visceral voices within grew, ran ahead of him, flooded his mind to bursting point. Younger versions of his wife and himself told him what should be happening. All had angry exchanges about betrayal, all bemoaning the fact that they had scrupulously followed the agreed plan.

How could their older selves have fucked it up so badly? Headaches flared up as these persistent internal voices ignored his pleadings for quiet. Internal animosity was never far away:

"It was her fault. You have been duped."

With no healthy way of working off steam, Martin went stir crazy. Any mysterious phone call to the flat was taken to be a lover quickly cancelling the call without speaking or making brisk excuses to get off the line. The sound of his internal voices and any unexplainable noises in the flat were causes of severe irritation. Pitiless never-ending self-torture was destroying any happiness to be found. Misery brought on by the chasm between unrealised desires and the impossibility of achieving them caused confusion between reality and illusion. The outside world had taken his wife and life away from him. The once shared worldview lay in tatters. What was an emasculated man supposed to do with his time? He had vivid daydreams of iconic looking men bursting out of fine suits, ripping off dull shirts and ties, ravishing his wife. Each one, with a crafty grin, leered at him while taking turns to make hay with his wife.

"Cuck-old, Cuck-old..."

He wanted to smash that fucking cuckoo clock.

****

One day, Martin went out, walked, jumped on a bus and got off at the terminus in a business park on the outskirts of town. It was a typical modern site, full of roundabouts and grass verges with the same fabricated blocks down each turn off, nothing special, where every turn off looked identical. The day was clear and bright as he roamed around. His wife worked on this site. He found the road signs confusing, only indicating the block number, not the company name. Everything around him was awash in bright light. After working up a sweat and apprehensive feelings, he eventually found what he was looking for. He was prying and knew the reaction it would cause. Unfortunately, his internal voices were no friends, guides or motivators; all of them had become despondent, mischievous and vindictive.

He stood before a unit rented out to the *Alpine Plastics Signage Specialists.* He quickly recognised their car. It was next to the *Herr Direktor's* VW estate. He knew this because of the reserved signs. The site layout consisted of a car park in front of an opaque glass double door entrance to what was essentially a large shed with a ground floor reception and upstairs offices tacked in front to it; very clean with dark frosted glass and aluminium sparkling in the sun, but all the same just a shed. On entering the building, the carpeted reception was straight in front of the visitor. On the right stairs went up to the office suites and on the left a plain set of double fire doors led to the open plan concrete floored factory. At the rear of this large workshop resided toilets, canteen facilities and a large goods entrance.

Today, everything was inside out. A strange jigsaw puzzle was coming together: the fairy tale world was real; good and evil existed as definable separate entities. The unit transformed into a twelfth-century stone keep where the hated baron was about to have his 'first night' with his fair maiden. As a gallant roving knight, he had to intervene, save the day. He was alert and ready for action. His body and skin felt firm and tight for the first time in a long while.

The metamorphosed Martin walked into the building where a happy smiling receptionist said good morning and asked him what she could do for him.

"Is your master at home?"

Assuming that this foreigner, probably English, was not fluent in her language, she politely compensated for his bad German by enunciating that he was in and would ring upstairs once she knew what he wanted.

Not waiting, *the hero* bounced up the stairs, two steps at a time. Once through the fire doors at the top of the landing, he was confronted with a narrow corridor providing access to four offices, a drinks area and a clerical staff only toilet. Easily recognising the director's door by its grandeur, his neck throbbed and loathing overwhelmed him. He walked straight in without knocking. Instead of seeing a bland office with a boring display of raw and finished samples of sheets and rods of plastic, Martin conjured up a dark hall suitable for a dastardly villain. The displayed samples became a wall full of swords and shields.

In front of him, sat the most unlikely imaginable villain: a small fat bald man that was more likely to be the slap on the head victim in a *Benny Hill* skit than a grandiose *Wagnerian* warlord. The man who knew everything about plastic sheeting and nothing about extra-marital affairs, with its furtive glances and lies that entwined the participants, was completely baffled when Martin advanced towards him. The concerned man used to the dignity and respect that his position gave him, thought something had got lost in translation. Lingering doubt did not last long as it was obvious that this unexpected intruder was crazy. Panic set in and *Herr Direktor* recoiled backwards in his castor swivel chair and hit the wide soundproof glass window that looked down on the factory floor. He became a frightened little boy.

"I demand satisfaction," cried Martin who then grabbed a plastic rod, using it as a rapier, flexed it, and whirled it above his head before pointing it at the retreating and very tensed up perceived love rival, a man naturally used to overact when confronted with everyday work mishaps.

"En Garde, you swine."

Meanwhile, bafflement filled the minds of the observing onlookers. Freddi, eyes fixed on her husband, frozen, stood at the connecting doorway with cups of coffee in her hands while the eyes of the workers on the factory floor pointed up at the high window. All of them watched as an unfit bigger man chased a little one round and round a large office desk. Faster and faster the two went, *Tasmanian devils*, one full sized and the other a cub in comparison. Martin worked himself into a frenzy, head shaking, and blood beating loudly in his ears. The bewildered stout little German just kept running, his arms and legs independently swinging and flailing. It had been a long time since this man's heart was required to pump faster than a sedate rate, probably when he had last had the urge to ravish his plump wife after drinking too much plum schnapps one distant Christmas day.

The love interest recovered from the state of shock that had temporarily paralysed her. She did not know if she should cry or be angry, instead she shot Martin a look:

"What are you doing?

You have gone completely berserk."

All the time Martin wacked the poor man on the back of the head or swished the rod along the desktop, knocking its accoutrement on the floor, only to be trampled on by the pursuer and the pursued. One of the first items to fly off the desktop was the family portrait placed there to remind the manager why he was here.

Freddi tried to put a stop to the proceedings by throwing the coffee into the face of her husband, only to miss and drown her waning boss in the face and neck with the hot liquid. Below all the workers had taken their eyes off the plastic sheets being moulded. The melting plastic turned to flames and black toxic smoke, setting off the fire alarm. The exhausted *Herr Direktor* and Martin had by this time collided and were hanging onto each other, breathing in sharp gasps, both wondered if they were experiencing a heart attack. The extra weight of Martin caused the other to lose his balance and slip into the glass pane of the factory floor-viewing window. The rattled window justified its safety glass sticker placed in the bottom corner of it by sustaining the joint weighted of the floundering pair. From below, it looked as if the boss was being throttled and the black coffee on *Herr Direktor's* shirt looked like blood pouring from his throat. From where Freddi stood, it brought back memories of late night drunkenness in Railhead. Violently trembling, she finally snapped:

"I want a divorce!"

Her shoulders heaved as she finally allowed herself to break down in tears and bolt away, down the corridor and out of the unit. The receptionist had already called site security and some workers voluntarily were making their way up to the office. In a matter of minutes, the intruder was manhandled, ruffled up, nose broken, dragged down the stairs and taken to the car park. The remaining alarmed and commiserating staff surrounded the dishevelled *Herr Direktor*.

Several police cars arrived when it was reported that a madman had rushed through the unit crying blue murder. The arrival of the fire brigade, sirens blazing, then added to the confusion. Their no-nonsense approach to dealing with fires in premises known to contain toxic materials spooked the gathered crowd. The firefighters simply barged through everyone and this unintentionally gave Martin an unexpected moment of freedom. It was all too much to bear for the *avenging hero* whose final last act of defiance before recapture was to vomit over the roof of the victimised man's car. A fast-flowing projectile made up of breakfast cereal, beer and stomach bile that emptied his guts.

As the police carted the deranged Martin off, burning with fever, foaming in the mouth as if shaken beer was gushing out of it and forcing saliva to run down the sides of his chin, all that was heard by the puzzled on-lookers was the incessant cries of

"Eddie Kidd... Eddie Kidd...Eddie Kidd..."

****

At the police station, as Martin bellowed to anyone that would listen that he had rights and demanded justice, the officers unhand cuffed the hooligan, put him in a straitjacket, threw him in a cell and waited for the arrival of an ambulance to take him away to the state hospital in *Emmendingen*.

The medics that wheeled him into the ambulance had seen it all before and had no time for any antics

so they firmly informed him that this was not
England and in Europe, where they made the rules.
They then proceeded to heavily sedate him to create
some peace to enjoy the views as the ambulance
drove deep into the Black Forest.

Sedated for days, Martin eventually woke up, red-
eyed, head throbbing, arms sore, naked apart from a
modesty gown with the overpowering smell of
disinfectant hitting his nostrils. Initially unfocused,
breathing deeply with his pulse racing, Adam's
apple bobbing up and down, and eyes far away,
terror naturally ran up and down his spine. If he
had pants on, they would have been soaked. The
sound of working electronics made him aware of
monitors plugged into his brain and arms. One was
an electroencephalogram to detect abnormal brain
activity. A female nurse hurried along spotlessly
clean polished floors into the room to see what was
happening. A loud beeping monitor had alerted her
that the patient was awake. After a quick check, she
phoned the shift supervisor of the news. Some
moments later, senior medical staff in white coats
gathered round him. He had always dreaded
hospitals, and then as his vision and awareness
improved, it became very apparent where he was.
Beethoven quietly playing in the background, bars
on the windows and strapped to the bed, it was the
loony bin or more correctly stated a psychiatric
institute for assessing the criminally insane.

In the beginning, Martin tried to elucidate what had
happened. However, no one wanted to listen to his
ravings as the correct diagnose required

independently gathered findings. The medical staff had tests to do and results to record and analyse. Like all humans, the doctors were primarily interested in labelling the behaviour of the subject in front of them from a specific perspective, their own. In nature, an entity exists in an unknown complex form then Man comes along and gives it a label. The label and how it was determined there forth hinders the complete understanding of it. In addition, the behaviour of the entity, in this case, the patient, was affected by the measurements and tests conducted on it.

Nevertheless, the repentant inmate tried to confess his moment of madness, said sorry and would not do it again:

"It was all too much for me. Living a life where my previous efforts felt unappreciated. All worsened by chronic illnesses. Not an inner mental struggle but a complete explosion of raging paranoia brought on by a rapid change in circumstances causing a fall in status, and no longer being required to be the breadwinner. Descent into madness not helped by the lack of a worthwhile daily routine and a distorted perception of what was going on about me.

See I understand!"

Even if anyone was listening, the outside world did not hear any coherent confession, only silly ravings as the voice coming out of him uttered inaudible mutterings and whimpers.

The gathered medical staff just continued with the preliminary inspections. Martin definitely did not like the feeling of awkwardness caused by the exposure of his willy to fully dressed strangers. Struggling to keep his emotions under control his despair grew. Seismic upheavals in the mind broke down all resemblance of a functional being. The beast within him would not stay quiet and once again won dominance. Trauma, derangement and acts of imbecility came to the fore. The spouting of loud feverish nonsense, gibberish and speaking in tongues, created all the classic signs of lunacy. His mind went blank and once again, the man had no idea where he was. The initial assessment stated that the patient was experiencing a catatonic episode. More thorough examinations were then proposed to determine the root cause of this state.

The institute checked him for all kinds of diseases and internal conflicts that could explain his irrational behaviour. Physiologists and pathologists looked for the presence of all known infections, vitamin deficiencies and metallic poisons linked to mental disorder. Neurologists checked for *Down syndrome*, atrophy and synaptic disorders. As a foreign national, the doctors also made sure that he was not carrying *TB* or *rabies*. In case the patient was a hapless drugs mole, his anus was examined for tell-tale signs of leaked cocaine. Because nothing physically wrong was found a mental dysfunction was assumed.

Next, it was the turn of the psychiatrists to resolve the issue, by trying to discover subconscious or buried emotional traumas for the bizarre outbursts. They wanted to know if the patient was a victim of abuse or a natural sociopath. Did he fit into the category of a schizophrenic, bipolar or borderline personality? Experimental drugs were pumped into him to see what effect these had. Even baby rattles and cute little teddy bears were waved in front of him to monitor any variation in his brainwave patterns.

Consideration was given to extracting a piece of his brain to put it through a meat grinder to look for signs of *CJD*. In the end, enthusiasm to find a medical cause faded as interest dwindled. The unresponsive patient befuddled them. If they could not ascertain what malady struck him then it was transparent that no cure could be found. Without a clear classifiable cause, Martin was continually passed around each specialist group in the hope of eventually establishing a reason. His medical case file got thicker and thicker as each department and expert entered their findings with *Verrücktheit* stamped across them.

For the patient and orderlies, probably ex-Stasi guards finding a new use for their skills, the rigmarole seemed endless. These orderlies had to wheel Martin in and out for all the sessions, stroll him round the secured grounds, wash him, make him take all types of different prescribed drugs and help with his toilet. These underlings did have fun with the English patient. When no one of authority was around, childish pleasure was obtained by repeatedly opening the viewing flap of the reinforced door to his cell. This action triggered the desired response from the starrily eyed loon, who spontaneously spurted out his trademark:

"Eddie Kidd, Eddie Kidd..."

Emaciated by dehydration, smelling of antiseptic with all his good bacteria wiped out, Martin did not feel good at all. All the treatments and probing just buggered up his natural constitution and fuelled his paranoiac tendencies. Lying regressed in the foetus position, spit dribbling down his jaw, he looked beaten, a shadow, full of soppy self-pity. A thousand times, he had swallowed his pride and said sorry for any hurt done. No one asked him how he felt. No one visited him to cheer him up or to tell him that everything would be all right. He had been miserable but was more miserable now.

The doctors finally admitted defeat and officially classified him as a hopeless case, completely gone, lost to this world. No one could find a box to tick that explained his condition and the standard course of therapeutic treatment associated with it. Like anyone caught up in a system that did not have a procedure for their specific needs, the patient was classified as an anomaly, a problem, caused by irreversible damage due to unknown psychological or physiology reasons. Of course, each specialist had their own conjecture with the English disease commonly known as excessive alcohol consumption not being one of them:

"It is not epilepsy."

"He is psychologically disturbed."

"He has suffered an irreversible breakdown."

"His brain has deformed under the strain and no amount of therapy will reverse the damage."

"Just murmurs repeatedly to himself."

"Completely passive to everything."

"He has an impregnable emotional block."

"Beyond hypnosis."

"His mind is chemically unbalanced with burnt out circuitry. He does not feel a thing when needles are stuck into him. No healthy behaviours seen at all."

"Our efforts to bring him round by gentle kind persuasion had no effect. Our communication attempts dismissed by his disparaging use of that irritating phrase."

"He is completely deranged. We have no way of establishing any doctor-patient trust. Probably concealed his dysfunctional thoughts for years, bottling up his feelings until he just exploded."

"There is no hope for him."

The doctors could not glean much insight into the breakdown from his upset and angry wife. It had been a mortifying experience for the woman that had filled her with nausea, left nerves frayed with

the shenanigans in the office seared into her mind
forever. She initially just said that it was as if he got
up one morning, decided to follow her to work and go
berserk. However, gentle guidance allowed a slightly
fuller picture to be painted. The doctor's report
indicated that she did not know precisely what to
think as she did not have the words to express her
feelings, but with appropriate coaxing managed to
state that her husband had been spending all his
time brooding away so self-absolution and loss of
propriety probably led to a warped mind. She had
actually used stronger language that was more vivid
and colourful but the doctor just wrote down a
cleaner version of her opinions.

In the additional comments section of this report, it
was recommended that psychological treatment be
made available to Freddi. Besides being extremely
pissed off, psychological scarring left her in a bad
place, not helped by the resulting gossip. The staff at
the factory having had expected a normal good
productive day spent the rest of that day and several
days after it while equipment was cleaned and
checked in blissful discussion about the English
loony and inferred accusations about the
relationship between *Herr Direktor* and his willing
office assistant. The workers' committee sent out a
formal rebut with a warning to end such talk, but,
despite getting some heart given support, Freddi
decided to pack her job in.

In the end, it was generally agreed to formally state
that the patient deliberately aimed to create as
much embarrassment for his wife as he possibly

could. The behaviour seen afterwards was a defence mechanism to divert blame and responsibility for his actions. In their opinion, the patient could not think of a rational explanation to justify his histrionic tantrums so just regressed backwards to evade responsibility. The hypersensitive chief financial administrator at the institute was not happy with this imprecise conclusion. The potential costs for indefinitely looking after a patient with possible idiopathic complications was not taken kindly. The spreadsheet forecasts indicated that the amount involved was staggering:

"The state had to be protected from bearing these types of costs for a foreign national."

Financial concerns were subsequently raised with *Baden-Württemberg* autocrats with a possible solution suggested. The regional overseers decided to approve the proposed recommendation, which was to discretely release the patient so saving them the trouble and expense. The excuse being it would be better for the patient before he became too dependent on the institution and seeing it as a permanent safe haven.

An immediate change of air would do him the world of good.

Ignoring the future possibility of self-harming, one early morning as dawn was about to break, an ambulance and a private car sped through pine trees, crossed the *Rhine*, and reached the nearby French border. The patient was transferred to his own car and a plain-clothed police officer drove him through an unmanned customs post. On the other side, the stolid officer stopped the car, got out, told Martin never to come back, and then swiftly walked across the border to his own side. With supreme efficiency, the authorities kicked the unwanted man out of Germany.

Martin had to quickly learn how to get through the coming hours, through the first one then the next and so on until he stopped thinking that he was mad; to a time when his mind would once again be consumed by daily life and the voices in his head faded back into the subconscious.

The last medical help provided was the gift of a large brown glass bottle containing non-alcoholic nerve-smoothing syrup with instructions to take one large swig after each meal. Enough was provided to see him reach England.

WAXING AND WANING

Besides the old jeep tank full of petrol, the German authorities reunited him with his clothes, passport and credit cards. Freddi, under advice from a solicitor, took what she was entitled from their joint savings accounts leaving the rest for him. There was enough left to start again, if not wasted.

For a couple of days, not surprisingly, the disoriented Martin felt like shit and drove shakily, trying to not pass out at the wheel. During this time, the jeep travelled not northwest but southwest towards *Lyon*. Doubts about his ability to survive troubled him and the need to rest was overwhelming. However, sleep did not come easy as adrenaline ran through his body, circulating within him causing a build-up of nervous excited energy and a pounding heart. In simple words, his metabolism was all over the place: fucked up.

On the first day of freedom, he stopped at a twenty-four-hour self-service roadside motel; vividly remembering the moment in front of the fully automated reception area with his rejected credit card in his hand with only one more go to get the security code right before the machine ate it. The correct sequence of numbers was either forgotten or had been nervously mistyped. Uncertainty flooded his mind. It was vital to get it right, just had to. It was only the reversed year of his birth after all. With great relief, the card was finally accepted. With the approved credit card came shelter, food and water in the form of a room, chocolate, croissants and plenty of coffee from the provided vending machines. After weeks of hospital food, it was delightful to taste real food again. He then spent the remainder of the evening violently throwing up followed by a restless disturbed night in a bland pale room that was too hot with walls that bowed and a ceiling that bore down onto him.

He waxed and waned, spluttering and stuttering for a few days until his tongue and vocal cords regained functionality as his stomach settled and the digested nutrients started to aid him. From vending machine food, he moved onto bottled beer while munching *baguette aux frites* and *poulet roti*. Nagging pains, bad dreams and disrupted sleep eased as the effects of the drugs wore off and the smell of confinement left him.

As was always the case, the people first meet were

the ones that coloured the impression of a place. He had stopped at *Mâcon*, met some nice kind people and decided to stay for a while. For most outsiders, the town was just a place to stop for a couple of hours or spend a night after travelling all day. Its main and outstanding feature was a centre that ran along a quay facing the wide expanse of the *Saône*. However, for the surrounding communes, the town served as the main commercial and administration hub. All the needs of a modern society obtained in one place as agricultural life continued outside the town's boundary.

Martin went native. Re-entering a world full of clear bright light and avoiding dark places helped with his recovery and understanding, allowing him to take responsibility for his breakdown. The world continued regardless of any wish to get off. The need to engage in it emphasised the natural fact that man was a social animal, not born to be alone. Everyone sought positive affirmation of his or her place in the world; it provided motivation to continue. Engaging in life forced him to apply his mind to external tasks and stop focusing on himself. It helped him to forget. If every small detail were remembered, he would surely go mad again. Torments about the biological imperative to leave genes behind came across silly when clearer reflection reminded him how imperfect all humans were. Maybe, all species were hard-wired to self-destruct, to prevent them from dominating the planet and destroying nature itself. The great plan laid seeds of self-extinction within everything.

Moving away and changing lifestyle did not bring complete relief but it did allow him to see how silly his existence had become. Complete exculpation did not exist in the real world and the residue of the past hung over him to cloud his vision. At night, his mind laid traps in his dreams to query previous decision-making and destructive acts. In these early days, persistent flashbacks illuminating his wild behaviour against that poor old man crumpled beneath him had made him cringe and filled him with embarrassment and guilt. At least no self-abuse or serious physical harm had been done. He made the most of his mind when it was not sluggish with any detected signs of depression doggedly fought against. The past few years had been a nightmare but the acquisition of a health-giving outdoor job provided further assistance to improve his countenance. Older, weaker and wiser, he learnt to believe some of his night time thoughts and dismiss others as a trick of the mind to unsettle him. Encumbrances that had hung over him gently slipped off his shoulders and good days arrived and were enjoyed to the full.

Hindsight was a great thing: react first then think later, it was the way of Man. What the fuck had he been thinking of; he had completely lost the plot, gone crazy and ruined a winning situation by being unduly suspicious. At least from now on, he tried to look on the bright side. Every husband at some point must have contemplated throttling his wife, an extreme form of *S and M*; a family snuff movie. Few, according to statistics, carried out such thoughts. Luckily, Martin did not become one of these statistics. Many different possibilities not seen at the time presented themselves to him. It did occur to him that Freddi would still be with him if richer outsiders had not priced them out of the market for a property in *Brettengen*. Although convinced that the root of his breakdown had been stress related, the place where it surfaced was avoided. Accordingly, he never returned to Germany, thought it wise to keep away, however, he never born any rancour with the country that held many fond memories for him.

His body aged considerably over this period. His long flowing hair was long gone with its loss blamed on the drugs injected into him at *Emmendingen*. A balding forehead and extended hairless temples now framed his parched stumbled face. What hair was left was permanently tied back into a thin streaky short lifeless grey ponytail. His stature was that of a stout stiff individual, usually cladded in heavy weather worn dusty black leathers with white and red trimmings as he had taken to motorcycling again; safe cycling on a sturdy second-hand *BMW cruiser* with good storage space. The old jeep was sold after his new abode was furnished. Driving in a metal cage had become claustrophobic, a new affliction attributed to his confinement in the psychiatric institute. Besides physical changes, a fair chunk of his cognition competency had been lost. The sharpness and quickness of thought once possessed was gone. Seeing the world through softer eyes, being less critical and trying to find the funny side when his intuition let him down compensated for the mental decline, he became more human.

Martin initially rented a small flat in town while arranging to buy a property outside of it. This flat was near a café-bar he frequented, a place that welcomed him. His diet was kept simple, eating and drinking the same as everyone around him. The English snobbish obsession for vintage was weird when offered the local riches. The only regular consumption not from the vicinity was the keg beers shipped in from *Alsace* and the French ports. Unsurprisingly the cash-rich Martin was a welcomed sight for the *notaires* with a suitable property soon found for him, and more importantly at a good price.

It was an old white-washed farmhouse with red tiles within a couple of acres of land located in an out of the way spot but it served its purpose: a retreat with good open views. It had been previously a family home and the remnants of the activity of young children were still visible. There was a protected outdoor playpen next to vegetable and fruit plots. The *notaire* explained that the owners had moved out for the sake of the children; returned to the city to get access to good educational facilities. They had kept a sheep that doubled as a family pet to keep the grass short. Classifying it as livestock allowed the claiming of livestock rebates. Martin kept up the same arrangement after this advantage was explained. An unexpected bonus of possessing a sheep soon became apparent; it provided good therapy. It was a good listener and never rebuked him, a white-coated creature that did not force him to take pills or cold showers. Their morning chats got the day off to a good start:

"Blah."

"It is a bit breezy."

"Blah."

"Yes, we just have to get on with it."

"Blah".

"You have discovered the meaning of life but no one wants to listen. Welcome to planet Earth."

An oddity of the place was a man-made hole about ten metres from the back of the house, fenced off with a low-lying length of rope. The previous owner was apparently a keen angler. Fish caught in the *Saône* had been thrown into it, left to mature, and ate when the family fancied some fish. A hosepipe of running water had maintained the water level and helped to oxygenise it. Considering there had been kids running around, it looked like an unsafe arrangement. Martin knew something about digging from his labouring days in Germany and was suitably impressed by the construction of this deep void. What was visible of it had dried out into smooth hard clay but what lay at the bottom was hard to tell. For all he knew it could have been a gateway to the underworld.

Spending was kept under control by not allowing the house to become a money pit. This not only saved money but also ensured nothing was done to harm its rustic character. Most houses in the *canton* had a falling down charm about them and his house would be no different. He had a go at gardening and found it enjoyable. An attempt at creating compost using kitchen waste and pulled weeds was abandoned. A sharp withdraw from this initiative occurred when snakes taking advantage of the free heat made their presence known. The nearest human settlement was to be found in a hamlet down the hill, a good long walk along an unlit single-track asphalt road. The small café-bar attached to the only shop was not the chattiest place in the world; nonetheless, everyone knew each other's business.

Missing out as much detail as possible, he got round to writing to Jason by addressing the letter to his mother's house to inform him of his new circumstances. However, it was Steve who had not been seen for years that popped in a couple of times before disappearing altogether again. Martin was a good host with a house stocked with booze of all types. The friends met long enough to discover what both had been doing and how Jason was getting on. His visitor was married, had a child, and doing surprisingly well, and now lived in Italy. Jason, according to Steve, had become a bore to be with, completely insular, a provincial, lost to this world.

To get some air, the pair ambled down to the hamlet's bar and drank for several hours, watched all the time by the proprietor and locals that came and went. One time, Steve asked Martin if *Saint Bartholomew* was the patron saint here. The question seemed strange to a distracted Martin:

"Why do you ask?"

"Oh, I overheard a couple of the old timers say '*salut au Saint Bartholomew*'."

"Maybe, he is."

"They do look like a backward lot, full with guilt if you go by the number of offerings left at that cross outside. You better watch yourself or you will end up burnt at the stake."

Steve then proclaimed that these types of communities were in for a shock:

"There are one hundred thousand Asian shopkeepers across the channel biting at the teeth to conquer this land."

On the way out, Steve would always look in the glass tray used to display tobacco. It was impossible to buy such out-of-date packets of cigarettes, cigars and matches anywhere else. This shop was a time capsule. An art-décor enthusiast would have instantly acquired the advertising plates, tray and its contents.

The friends generally talked about the old days, saw the funny side of life, and laughed at the stupidity of some past actions while quietly accepting that there probably would be more such actions in the future.

"Who would have thought all those years ago that we would have ended up living in mainland Europe," both exclaimed.

Like it or not, imperfections were what defined

them, made them friends and, anyway, their quirks had advantages as well as weaknesses.

On the way back, the young and the old of the commune noticed the jovial pair. The infants in the small school playground became still when the strange verbal utterings reached them. Old women stared at the unknown faces that glided past kitchen windows. Even the wall lizards looked more bemused than normal when the Englishmen walked passed them.

Martin was no longer a huddle jumper trying to clear fences in a race without an end. His job as a postal worker was not taxing and got his face known. The unsocial early morning starts did not faze him; the walking improved his fitness; helped his back and allowed long afternoons to be spent outside. Insofar as was possible, free time was made his friend and not the enemy. Rarely getting mail he clearly remembered the day in the sorting office when filling his sack to discover registered mail in the form of a large brown envelope addressed to him, it contained divorce proceedings to finally put a line under that part of his life. It was amazing how officialdom could find you when it desired. Communication between the solicitors produced an amicable separation, primarily due to Martin accepting all but a few terms of the settlement offered. That shared journey together had formally ended with the paying of the bill. Some months later, a crate arrived with his share of the goods, belongings that he insisted on retrieving; items that would be deemed necessary essentials for living on a desert island. It contained, records, books, tools and a small Edwardian wooden inlaid box once owned by his father. After being told off by Betty, he had gone and bought back his father's medals from the house clearance dealer.

****

A long peaceful period followed. His main haunt was still the bar in town, *Chez Pierre*. It was close to the post sorting office and offered a relaxing hour after work. The bar owner was an aproned wearing merry man with white hair and a bushy white moustache who always welcomed Martin by asking him if he was enjoying life. The regular talking companion for the proprietor at that time of day was the owner of another bar, located down a side street that only opened at night. This bar owner was a jowly thick-bearded ex-seamen who bought the concern as a pension. It was the town's lesbian hotspot managed by his large strong-willed wife. This old seaman's only experience of England was *Teesside*; sent there when the company he worked for wanted him to learn the international language. He always bemoaned that silly decision, as everyone in the ranks knew the best place to be sent was the company's site in *Caithness* where a clear slowly delivered English was spoken. When Martin was out at night, the old seaman would sometimes invite him to walk down to his bar and have free drinks on him. The world-weary man did not like drinking alone in his own bar. *Chez Pierre* was a bright cheerful emporium compared to this shadowy private drinking den. Whether by design or accident it had a ramshackle resemblance to a lower deck found in an old wooden galleon. It was hard to believe that the bar raised any income to support the owners in old age, as there was a distinct impression that the regulars were more interested in chatting than drinking. The unenthusiastic proprietor had a downer on women:

"On the seas where many a strange sight were seen, I dreamt of getting back on dry land and owning my own bar. Wishful thinking. Here, life has turned upside down since feminism, become more unsettled, aggressive and violent. Who is going to have the babies that a country needs?"

The old sailor observed how Martin's French had improved. Always quick to tell him never to bother about being criticised for speaking bad French as every region thought only its inhabitants spoke proper French.

"If you can make people understand you and you get what you want then you speak good French. Regional as well as national chauvinism was rife, a bit like England."

At night, customers at *Chez Pierre* were mainly early thirty-somethings drinking lager and possessing that natural French ability to appear, without trying, arrogant and confident. During the day, it was the home of workers escaping paid labour. Men dressed in blue overalls or the whites of kitchen staff and painters. These regulars drank coffee, *pastis* and wine and they received Martin into their group so bestowing the benefits of good DIY advice, cheap goods and services onto him.

Martin mainly spoke to two of these men. A mix of English and French was spoken to a Belgium dogsbody who worked in the hotel across the road. To gain acceptance at the bar, this northerner tolerated the inane ignoramus jokes about Belgium stupidity. In return, this man liked to moan about his work, in particular, the tight-fisted patron who allowed nothing to be thrown away, even the remains of half-eaten leftover side salads were rinsed under the tap and served again.

Only one language was spoken to the hard to please Benoit, a viniculturist, who knew no English and refused to learn it. It was hard to believe that this man was a viniculturist, as his appearance was more like that of an oil-soaked car mechanic. Benoit was hard to understand because of the possession a particularly strong nasal speech, and the habit of making strange inflexions when talking as if his inner workings were composed of moving mechanical parts. It had to be said that many a native found the mechanical rumblings of Benoit difficult to comprehend as well.

Benoit always spat when annoyed about something. It may have been true that what you did not want was what was required, but life had become overly complicated in the eyes of Benoit. Mention politicians and he would think of taxes and spit. They were just a bunch of peddling salesmen selling pipedreams to fools buying into ideas without substance. The independent principalities around the borders of France enraged him for being parasites that fed off larger nations:

"These places are tax avoidance domains for the rich.

Taxes should be gathered from everyone and only spent on the children and the old.

Some may sound sincerer than others but all politicians are slimy self-righteous conniving bastards."

A particular pleasure for him was to challenge everything others would say. He put down Martin's improvement in speaking his language by dismissing the pride that Martin expressed when told that another customer at *Chez Pierre* had asked Martin what part of France he came from. The sceptic just shrugged his shoulders and replied that this person obviously came from *Paris*, a fool who knew nothing about life outside the capital.

"People like that made the big decisions without any understanding how people lived outside the ivory towers of the capital."

Martin found out the mystery behind the rumblings that afflicted Benoit's speech when invited to see the winery and taste its latest batch. It was situated down a couple of side streets on a lane full of artisan sheds. The closer one approached the most greased stained shed of all, the greater the impression was given of a living creature huffing and puffing behind

the not so firmly locked wooden entrance doors. A
quick yank on a chain permitted the doors to swing
open to reveal a filthy spider infested garage
containing an aging *Citroën Acadiane*, antiquated
machinery and several large wooden vats. Along the
ceiling, pipes held up by sting and bits of chain went
one way then the next. The liquid within pumped by
a diesel engine that must have been at least forty
years old. The pipework huffed, rattled and hissed
from a hundred places. It was not clear why a
winery would have such a powerful pump and so
much piping running along the ceiling, but it had.
All made up of bits and pieces of salvaged machinery
reused to create someone's dream; probably that of
Benoit's father, and lovingly maintained by his son.
It was a testament to the maintenance skills of
Benoit that this enterprise was kept functioning.

Part of the viniculturist's joy was foraging for
replacements rather than to buy a substitute part.
On his rounds, Benoit would look out for abandoned
machinery, stop his van and spend twenty minutes
reclaiming anything that might be useful. He got as
much thrill in finding a rare sized bolt for the
restraining bracket on the pump as a woman would
find a matching handbag for her best jacket.
However, the biggest astonishing thing was hearing
the same random mechanical noises that manifested
from Benoit. The machinery and this poor man's
viniculturist spoke the same language.

The enterprise existed by swapping grapes for wine.
Benoit travelled round in his van picking up bins of
grapes from small holds and gardens. Each

negotiation involved debating how much wine would be given in return for the quality and quantity of grapes received. Each transaction was marked down in a greasy notebook with a copy given to the grape vendor. Benoit produced two types of table wine, a red and white one. No bottling or labelling was involved. The grape vendor would turn up on the agreed day with his own containers to receive his quota. The tap on the vat would be opened for the appropriate amount of time that corresponded to the agreed amount of litres. Experience had taught Benoit that ten seconds of running wine was roughly equivalent to a litre. What remained in the vats after each contributor received the amount allocated to them belonged to Benoit to sell to the general public. If you could manage to get Benoit engaged in conversation while the taps were open then you always got more than your entitlement.

Afterwards, the public turned up and paid a rate appropriate for the quality achieved for that batch. The classification of each batch would be clearly stated on a chalkboard. It would either be drinkable, fine or good. The wine would be poured into jugs, bottles or small barrels. It all depended on what the customer provided. Benoit never knowingly sold a bad wine, nonetheless, it was what it was: a young fruity wine to be drunk immediately. Its shelf life was less than heat-treated supermarket milk. Martin would sometimes go out in the van to help collect the bins, deliver wine and gather tips on the best places to forage for firewood, wild herbs and fruit. The stove at home required feeding and free fuel always came in handy. Sawn chunks of felled trees, old vines and damaged pallets from factory yards all made the way back to *Chez Martin*. Even a discovered rusty horseshoe found a new home above the front door of the house. When time permitted it a bit of fishing was enjoyed. If a customer gave Benoit enough notice then other items were willingly collected and passed on from one customer to another. It was on one of these trips that a young ewe was saved from the slaughter. From that day onwards, every day was a bonus of the animal, soon to be spoilt and turned into a barrel-shaped coarse furred creature with a comical whimsical small head, standing on scrawny black legs.

La Roche de Solutre dominated the landscape on some of these meandering journeys through the *cantons* around *Mâcon*. A reminder that man had been in this region since prehistoric times when the summit was used to drive wild horses to their deaths onto the rocks below. Under Roman control, the region became famous for its wine growing and as a gateway to the north.

A drinker that sometimes frequented *Chez Pierre* was known as the *Count*, the inheritor of a dilapidated chateau, which was opened up for summer fetes and garden parties. Every couple of years a reservoir in the estate was drained to allow guests to wade in and gather up fish to cook on a makeshift barbecue. He had taken the old jeep off Martin's hands to use as a run around on the estate. His family had their own heraldry shield and the dusty threadbare tapestries hung precariously around the main rooms of the chateaux were a reminder of a once illustrious past. This cultured free-spirited cash-strapped aristocrat worked in winter as a handyman to leave his summers free for relaxation and travels around Europe. He possessed an aquiline nose with all the traits associated with it: tall, straight and *bon vivant*, an interesting character with no master or means to force anyone to do his bidding. Nonetheless, the man was venal as they come when given the opportunity. This middle-aged man was still a player. The *'joie de vie'* was written on his face, a face seen on many a young child whose mother kept a guilty secret. This irreverent and irrelevant modern-day aristocratic rascal still claimed his *'droit du seigneur'*, not just on the first night but the second and so on.

"A man cannot tickle himself. It is why celibate men are miserable bastards."

The *Count* and Martin would regularly chat when he delivered mail. Over a coffee or a cognac, the friendly pair discussed parts of Europe both had visited and the local history. This more in the brains than money in the pocket aristocrat knew where to find all the best bordellos: hotels with extra services assured. In his view, a beautiful woman should never find any trouble in eating or clothing herself. In many ways, the man liked being impoverished as it allowed him to live carefree without any pressure to take on an air of responsibility, which distinguished the serious-minded from the masses, whose company he preferred.

"You cannot study humanity in a dusty library, you

had to go out and live among it, and see the human condition for yourself. The best places to see it in all its glory are in the slums and brothels. The people there do not have the time or the inkling to put on false airs, their pettiness, stupidity and follies are all openly displayed."

Holding a cigarette in one hand and a glass in another, the *Count* would explain the nature and lineage of the local natives. Apparently, superstitious beliefs and inbreeding were ripe; cousins had been marrying cousins for generations and many family trees had interlinked complex entangled branches, causing a host of birth deficiencies and idiocies. His family was not excluded but he was philosophical about it:

"Inbreeding creates extremes with thoroughbreds produced alongside the lame and in the case of humans, highly intelligent people living among the imbecile and physically unattractive. When on your daily travels look around, the Neanderthal still exists here. Of course, I am a case of the former. My perfect face is a tell-tale sign of my superiority."

Sometimes after work, instead of heading straight to the bar, Martin went to the quay and watched the river flow. To the untrained or indifferent busy eye, all that was seen was reflected light and pools of dark water. With time and patience, this overcast patina dissipated to reveal the aquatic world below, a world with its own colour and sense of order where creatures followed the same paths as ancient ancestors. On quiet moments like this, Martin reflected. It dawned on him that being a postman was a good way of integrating into the community, gaining acceptance, doing something important and being part of the greatest gift that the creation of society had unintentionally created, a way to allow people to keep in touch and prevent isolation. The arrival of the post gave hope to people, bridged communities and spread news. Each morning on his rounds, most people were happy to see the mail van or his bike pull up in the anticipation of news or an awaited parcel. Cafés and restaurants in the early morning were more relaxed places where an offer of a free espresso was never far away. The office receptionist waited on the arrival of the mail and the offer of a hard-boiled sweetie was a big thank you. On his rounds, it was observed how town folk engaged in easy conversation when bumping into others who possessed something in common; a fishing rod in their hand or a dog on a lease. How countryside dwellers just waved to each other as rarely anything new had to be said; taciturn acknowledgment of their existence and place in the landscape sufficed.

Isolation was the worse form of psychological torture for a creature. Only an abnormal person, a psychopath, with emotional disconnect could endure prolonged separation. At least Martin knew that he was not on the extreme scale of human behaviour. His breakdown at *Emmendingen* and the symptoms suffered since that confinement underlined his normality. It led to the acknowledgement that looking for excuses or pity was not a cure, and admitting guilt should not be avoided, as understanding was what led to better mental health. Hiding and denial was the mark of the coward while a desire for the accumulation of wealth was a poor substitute for happiness if it led to isolation and made you insecure, needy or petty minded. *Weltechmerz* afflicted humanity and Man had to make the best of it. He was now able to recall some of the Buddhist sayings that his Karate instructors used to pronounce during training sessions:

"Purge yourself of selfish and evil thoughts, for only with a clear mind and conscience can understanding be received."

Our Leader was an unconscious creation to warn of the dangers of only given emphasis to the parts and not the whole. A robotic chemist distilling a substance to extract the compounds it only wanted, throwing away impurities: unwanted elements that provided stability.

Martin would sometimes wonder how his old friends were getting on. However, it never resulted in any correspondence with them. In many ways, it seemed pointless. There was no news, he had lost touch with the comings and goings in the land of this birth, and a settled existence was uninteresting when written down; all that could be said was 'still alive'.

Anyway, no one contacted him.

****

Nevertheless, the world was not full of people seeking enlightenment. It was packed with unhappy souls looking for scapegoats for the seismic disturbances around them. In this case, the influx of foreigners had affected the lives of the natives. Their *canton* was being opened up and taken away from them. Outsiders made it more expensive for their children to continue the existence their parents and grandparents enjoyed. To the natives who did not know him, Martin was a black and white example of such people and not seen as the bringer of good news and advancement but a destroyer of a way of life. A way of life that meant the forenames and surnames on the letters and parcels delivered were the same as those to be found in the local graveyard; a graveyard that was kept pristine and was visited at least once a week by a family member. Like all aboriginal cultures, a deep reverence for the dead and the land was held. The people knew how to maintain the land, kill for food and to eliminate pests. Silent intimation of the adults and peer bullying of their children at infant school had encouraged the previous occupants of the house at the top of the single-track road to abandon the place.

They got the message and so would Martin.

The *St. Bartholomew's Day* massacre was a purge, to halt change and limit choice. It was sanctioned by the monarchy to help keep its power but conducted by the canaille on others seen as being different, a threat. The slaughter started with the *Huguenot* leaders in *Paris* and expanded outward to the other regions and towns. At the end of two brutal unforgiving weeks, thirty thousand lay dead while the survivors fled to the lowlands and England.

Ironically, *Bartholomew* was canonized to sainthood for also being a victim of a tyrannical cruel state; the man was beaten, flawed and beheaded for his beliefs. Now, some disheartened young men from the hamlet, avid supporters of the national sporting teams, sat around a shaky table in the café-bar at the bottom of the road from where Martin lived. Apart from a well wrapped up old woman serving behind the counter, passing the time knitting and watching a muted TV set, the bar was theirs. Her customers had been drinking wine all day and had watched the international rugby on TV. *Les Bleus* had lost to England, not lost but hammered and Saturday had been spoilt. Elbows on table, they cursed everything in sight. Not only did they all have a similar physical appearance and same distinct accent, tonight, all facial expressions were identical. It was as if one was surrounded by mirrors and saw multiple reflections staring back at him. The men were working themselves up into a fever. This was not too difficult to achieve, as by nature, all were clannish, vulnerable to rage and hard countryside living filled them with testosterone. All it took to ignite them was the addition of alcohol and the identification of a victim to de-humanise.

On a wall facing the drunks, a political poster campaigning for the previous *canton* elections fed them ideas. The poster portrayed *Liberté* in front of *Le Tricolore*, defending *la vième republique* against an unseen enemy as *Paris* lay in ruins. It called for action. *La Front National* was boldly displayed on the top of the colourful imaginary and the candidate named at the bottom. Just in case the message was not clear enough, someone had scrawled *La France Pour Les Francais* over the poster. The emotions stirred, patriotism ran through the veins of the drunken peasants to swell fearlessness:

"It is true something had to be done to protect our way of life."

"It is time for the talking to stop."

The spending spree of outsiders was seen as a cultural threat; house prices were forced beyond the means of the natives and rich city living was corrupting rural values. All this caused great resentment because they could no longer afford to live in the communities of their birth or live authentic lives without offending the urbane proclivities of these invading dwellers. These meddlers had the worse type of ignorance: arrogance and the assumption of always knowing what was best. All they talked about was artisan cheeses and the silly dress sense of the natives; glorified tourists gawking at them as if actors in a heritage enactment theme park while they were supposed to collaborate by beaming welcoming smiles and chattering inane salutations. The clothing of the natives had become the symbol of their diminished status in society, the lowest one in the technological age. Their contribution not appreciated and deemed irrelevant. Nonetheless, there was more to rural life than *le fromage Mâconnais*. Tradition required an understanding of the land. These outsiders adored the smoked wild boar meats but were offended by the killing of them.

As the night wore on, the wish to assert the right to exist grew stronger. Spitting out prejudices and exploding into nonsensical rants, circular rebellious arguments cascaded round the wine-stained table. The shouting, the banging of fists and unanimous agreements turned them into a herd of fully clothed crimson beasts. Nothing was enigmatic about these natives. Nothing astute was said, no clever sophism, just outspoken hatred and frustration of their powerless existence. Why did things have to change when an uncomplicated lifestyle could suffice? The people should rise up and do what the Welsh had done: burn them all out, every single one of them, until there was no more room left in hell. Instead of condemning the urban middle and liberal classes for forcing advancement and opportunities for themselves without due regard for others, the bar room talk turned to direct action against a close at hand target. It was settled that the happy smiling postman should be the first to feel their revenge. Every morning this cuckoo in the nest scared the chickens and disturbed the milking by worrying the cattle. The fact, that this unpretentious man would have agreed with the sentimental assessments being expressed and would have swelled the ranks to preserve their way of life never occurred to any of them.

 "Let's smash the windows of that bastard up the hill."

"Better than sitting here."

"Anyway, this wine is shit."

"Nothing to fuck here either."

As the herd of Gadarene swine mustered outside, the lights on the side of the shop that housed the bar switched off after the old woman lethargically got off her seat, lifted the glasses off the table, wiped it clean with a damp cloth and headed upstairs.

Fuelled by ignorance and indifference to the lives of others not to mention the alcohol, up the road the revolt of peasants staggered, sharing a bottle of cognac on the way, gathering up sticks and stones, their ramble rousing audible to anyone in the hamlet wanting to listen or find out what was causing the commotion. However, the place remained comatose. If they had torches and pitchforks their appearance would have been straight out of a *B horror movie*, where the peasants finally had enough and were hell-bent on freeing the village from a hideous monster housed in the high perching castle.

The air was fresh and sharp. The topsoil crunched under feet whenever one of them drifted off the road. Away from the hamlet, the trees camouflaged them. The world became darker and colder as the men wrapped their jackets up tight. Moonlight reflected off freezing puddles in ditches and frosting asphalt. The surrounding wood was breathing. The hard boots hammering the road awoke crows and magpies. The shirking, yelping and the shuffling of branches indicated the recommencement of a turf war. Apart from the seed carriers and the pollinators, all other organic life forms were parasitical here. In revenge the wood had created hidden traps to trip the weary, to leave them exposed, injured, to die of hyperthermia or starvation.

Advancing up the hill, hesitation entered some of their minds. The wraithlike undulations of what seemed to come from a deranged animal within the wood haunted the quietened mob, whose enthusiasm ebbed with the lowering of body heat. The heathen must be performing some devilish act forcing the wood to close in on them. Ten unsettling minutes into the impromptu campaign as a bright starry sky opened upon them, the muffled sound of heavy rock reached the ears of the attackers before sighting glimpses of a well-lit house when the cypresses became sparser along the side of the road. The monster was taunting them by polluting the countryside with Anglo-Saxon howling. The ground beneath their feet felt as if it was pulsating to a beat they did not want to follow.

At the top of the rise, the glare from *Mâcon* could be seen tainting the night sky, creating a reddish haze that contrasted with the shadowy outlines of distant hills and the dark coppices scattered between the vineyards. The white and red points of light that flickered along hidden roadways identified homeward bound traffic. On the left the remanent of the wood continued, behind it, a large sloping paddock housed goats and sheep belonging to the landowner below on the other side of the hill. In the small field on the right, the illuminated house of the outsider looked as if it was calling out to the world, a beacon of light and sound showing the way to a land of plenty and easy pickings. This sight alone rekindled the desire of the shivering rabble to cause mischief. Male bravado took over again, as they, all tried to outdo each other. Cries of *La Marseillaise* accompanied banging of sticks on a metal gate with a sign roped to it denoting the land as private property and a request to keep the gate closed.

"Onward friends, onwards."

"Cut the throats of the foreigners."

"Rejoice in the sight of the dying enemy."

At the same time, completely unaware of the approach of the late night uninvited visitors, Martin was happily playing air guitar in his front room as a *Black Sabbath* anthem blasted out of the stereo speakers. The rhythms and melodies of the loud music released memories of perceived long gone good old days. It was a night of wallowing in self-indulgence after having one of his good days: he too had been drinking far too much, but it was a soul raising one that came when in a nostalgic mood.

As was his habit on a day off work, Martin had risen early to enjoy the stillness of the morning, stillness emphasised by winter. Adorned in the local garb of thick two-piece blue dungarees with a matching cloth cap, clothes and boots obtained for virtually nothing from a fellow drinker at *Chez Pierre*, he roamed round the perimeter of his field under the pretext of looking for damage to the fencing but

really to see the retreat of nature. It was fascinating
how it closed down, withdrew, leaving the land to
Man. The only sounds to be heard were that of
blackbirds and rooks with the occasional lonely
proud red chested robin trying to be heard, uttering
its despondent trill.

After a late breakfast, the plots were tidied up. They
contained nothing fancy just mostly veg and some
fruit bearing bushes that looked after themselves.
At this time of year, nothing had to be done in the
fruit beds but winter vegetables, mainly brassicas,
required his nursing skills and a bit of weeding in
return for a cabbage and some leeks. That week's
rubbish was then bagged and put in the bin next to
the gate. These mundane routine activities coaxed
his mind into activity. With dirtied hands, the
feeling that the land and he were one gave him
pleasure, and set him up for the day, a day of
leisurely pursuits. He rode into town, watched the
river flow, headed to the bar for a coffee and cognac,
and after a bit of banter went to a supermarket to
buy bottles of *Pelforth Brune*, *pain au lait* and a jar
of *confiture de fruits* as weekend treats to go with
Benoit's wine. Happy to avoid going out for the rest
of the day, the all-weather biking gear was hung on
pegs in the kitchen as he relaxed in a tee shirt,
jumper and jeans. To keep the house warm logs
were placed in the fireplace and burnt.

Outside, in lieu of just throwing stones and insults
then running away, a curiosity developed on what
was happening within this hermitage so a decision
was made to creep through the field towards a

window thick with condensation. A sudden pause in the music stopped the trespassers in their tracks before the recommencement of the same cd invited them to continue their investigation. The window to gaze into was easily marked out by a fluctuating shadowy figure that indicated movement. Once amassed at the window, apart from an expensive looking Hi-Fi, everything was what would have been found in any other house: sturdy furniture and a roaring fire to keep the cold out. On the table was a jug of wine, a half-full glass of white wine and a discarded plate with the recognisable remains of a stew of garlic sausages and greens. The prancing Martin never noticed the enraged faces screwed against the window to get a better view through the grey mist that formed on the glass.

It was hard to believe that any animosity could be aimed at this inebriated jester. Nevertheless, unluckily for him, he had inadvertently drawn attention and suspicion. The happy recluse was about to find out again how quickly a hard-earned right to live could crumble about him. His life of monotone serenity, free of artificial distractions and the woes of others was coming to an abrupt end.

The gathered mob could not back down. It was too late to turn back, as any weakness in resolve triggering expression of uncertainty would cause the pack to turn against the waverer. The intruders made their way to the back of the house, instinctively expecting the kitchen door to be unlocked, by assuming the code of the countryside ruled here and an open door was always available to a distressed traveller, especially in stormy weather. Some managed this manoeuvre without difficulty; others by a roundabout route entangled themselves on the roping that separated off the dug hole. They soon regrouped and trooped inside. Familiar smells and heat from the stove hit them.

Head down, strumming harder with the sound of dominant guitars emanating from the speakers, the joyful house owner was oblivious to the world. This allowed the bemused rustics to wander round him without causing any alarm. When Martin became aware of the presence of others his self-inflicted dizziness combined with drink made him imagine that the forest trolls had decided to join the party by forming a circle round him, waiting to be asked to dance with him. When the reality of danger finally registered, the hallucination cleared and lucidity hit him:

"What the fuck!"

Stumpy broad nosed hardy looking young men with the same dark figures and clothes had surrounded him. The only thing to mark the intruders as being part of the modern world was a glimpse of an *Adidas* tee shirt beneath a loose overcoat. Otherwise, the same dress sense could have been seen in old sepia photos.

It was only a matter of waiting to see when the first blow was struck with the assailant remembered in folklore as a hero, a brave man; the man who stood up against the swarm of foreign invaders. The

scuffle began when one of them, standing behind
Martin, socked him with the easily within reach
wine jug. It did not smash but unbalanced him long
enough to encourage the others to wade in. The
much older man was caught in the middle of a
violent maelstrom as the muscle-bound thugs bored
down on him. An attempt at self-defence failed
miserably. Alcohol and decline in agility led to an
ineffectual attempt to land a nerve-crippling blow.
Undeterred the gnarled faced scum proceeded, in a
frenzied attack maintained by blind fury, to kick
him repeatedly until their irk against the outside
world was satisfied. One of them grabbed the stereo,
pulled it away from its electrical socket and
smashed it over the slumped scapegoat. The ferocity
eventually eased with each of them then taking
turns to wander over to give him a swift kick in the
ribs when any sign of life was shown.

In between drinking his booze, directing verbal
abuse at him and smashing his records, they
debated what to do with the sprawled-out victim.
The decision was to drag him out of the house and
throw him into the pit that some of them nearly fell
into. Ignoring the groaning as blood poured from his
mouth and nose, they treated Martin like a dead
weight of no value. His head banged against the
floors and doors then scraped on the outside gravel
path. Some futile resistance by blindly swinging out
his arms in the hope of catching one of the bastards
ceased when pain shooting from his badly bruised
ribs and pounded sinews proved too much for him;
constricting his breathing and forcing him to accept
his fate. The rancid remains of unlucky rodents,

desiccated fish and drowned snakes awaited his company.

Thrown into the pit, elbows jarring against its sides, Martin quickly hit the bottom. The shock from hitting water and the resulting pain from his back, legs, arms and sides encouraged him to stir. It was hard to move but it had to be done, he had to get out of the water. Pushing his body up to stand upright, his right ankle and ribs then also complained: the former was badly sprained and some of the latter felt cracked. For a few moments, the trapped man just stood, shaking and dazed, trying to remember what had just happened while taking everything around him in. The confined space revealed a sinister and foreboding character. There was not enough room to stretch his arms. A strange deathlike smell hung all around him. The heat of his body seeped out of him as he tried to listen carefully to catch the gist of the assailants' loud chatter. However, little was understood as it only came across as drunken rubbish and nonsensical ramblings.

Above him, shadowy faces peered down on him, all expressed amusement in one form or another as they gloated about what had just been done. Mocking laughter and projectiles then rained on him. Some of the assailants even relieved themselves. All Martin could do was lean down again, bend his knees and cover his head under his arms to let his shoulders and top of the spine take the brunt of the bombardment. When gravel was tossed down at him, some of it managed to get through his arms to smack the back of his head. The onslaught ended when the weather came to his aid. The cold wind blowing across the exposed field defeated any remaining willingness to spend any more time around the pit, especially when it was remembered that the house contained booze. Bizarrely, Martin learnt something new when one of the withdrawing thugs was heard to say:

"No shame in pissing in a crap hole."

The pit was an old privy left open when a previous owner had made modern sanitary improvements. Martin had also worked out the identity of the attackers. Not roaming motorcycle maniacs looking for a night's fun, nor escaped convicts looking for shelter, and definitely not rampaging animal rights activists mistaking him for an evil hunter. Their accents and grumpiness told him they were from the *canton*. They must have had often walked or drove past him; worse still, some had sometimes passed the time of day with him when delivering the mail.

With both puffed up eyes pointed upwards, Martin staggered to his feet again by pushing his sore back against the slimy collapsing wall as his feet slipped in the mud below the murky water. Smeared blood and swollen black eyes, contrasted with his pale complexion. It went unnoticed that his nose was broken again. Drenched in perspiration and muck, his hands shook, body shivered and his heart felt has if it was about to explode. Frantic attempts to try to find firm holds in the walls was a pointless waste of effort, it only exhausted him. Lack of exercise, damaged limbs and aging caused muscle spasms and intense pain in his ribs, arms, legs and neck as he tried to stretch upwards.

His earthy worries had a new priority. Instead of metaphysically worrying about being trapped by the finitude of time, confined physical spaced had imprisoned him. He had dug himself out of one hole to then be put into another one.

Claustrophobic terror embraced him and made him violently sick. The only way to diminish this anxiety was to maintain an upward gaze which did not help his neck or back. It was a horrendous situation to be put in. One action to mitigate discomfort led to an excruciating pain elsewhere; creating a slow agonising death similar to the torment endured by crucifixion. To make the situation even more comparable the suffering from his ribs must have been close to that produced when a Roman prisoner was flagellated. The height above him to the surface took on *Mount Everest* proportions.

The weather now turned for the worse with the arrival of low-lying black cloud. The darkness pressed down from above as droplets of rain got larger and closer together, and then it came down in opaque sheets. The downpour of sleet and rain caused the wall of the pit to become a barrier of slime. A renewed attempt to hoist out of the pit failed. The boost in energy from the result of panic and the will to live was uncoordinated and inevitably wasted. Fear only benefited the cause that manifested it. Trembling hands and slippery

soil also did not make good bedfellows. His fingers
felt broken and completely useless after scraping
away at the walls to try to reveal firm roots or large
secured stones to allow some grip. The thick woollen
jumper that kept him warm in the house was
soaked, heavy and detrimental to him. The jeans
clung to his skin, robbing him of heat by conduction.
His struggles left him breathless; not helped by
blocked sinuses and a dry mouth filled with the
taste of blood from the earlier brutal encounters. In
the darkness and the dampness of the pit, the fight
for survival would have deserted the strongest of
men. The irony for Martin was that if this incident
had occurred several years before, it would probably
have been accepted as his fate, happy to gain relief
from the sickness called existence. However, he had
found a new desire to get on with life. Defiance re-
surfaced and renewed attempts made to climb out,
only to once again fail, leaving his hands and
shoulders in even more pain.

His murder would be an otiose act. It was a
reminder that the death of an individual to prevent
the destruction of a way of life under threat from
progress was futile. Any death of a scapegoat was
only ever a personal catastrophe, nothing more. The
silence and his thoughts were interrupted by the
cries of drunken assailants or their disturbances as
the house was ransacked. The sound of footsteps on
gravel signalled the appearance of one of them at
the pit to ensure that the captive was still being held
and to empty his bladder.

Although, he felt bloody awful, dazed, frightened,

sick and in pain, the inclement weather, an inundation perhaps, illogically raised his spirits before the fatality of the situation once again swamped him. It was a silly false hope to expect the waters to rise up and overflow from the pit. It had never happened before so why should it happen now. Above him, all was quiet. The ransackers had drunken themselves to sleep, leaving all of the lights blazing in every room of the house. The cold and misery of a winter's night left to invade the house through left opened doors and smashed windows. As for Martin, tiredness and mental exhaustion followed the realisation that his future was outside his own control. It felt as if this forgotten man was a million miles away from any help. However, the need for hope was too powerful and caused him to hopelessly listen for any human sound that might signal a rescue. Surely, it was not impossible that something would happen to cause aid to arrive: a passing car glimpsing something odd or unsocial noise attracting the attention of some gendarmes.

His stomach and bowels made it known that contained contents had to be discharged. He crouched down with his jeans and pants pulled down to his thighs. His rear held just above the muddy water, as a jet of brown soupy liquid spurted out of his backside. The expelled contents swilled on the surface of the murky water. The initially obtained pleasure and brief comfort as his bladder and bowels emptied was short lived. The smell and thought of the additional filth around him quickly dispelled any euphoria. The pit was a quagmire of mud, human waste, blood from Martin's wounds along with the usual residents of rancid corpses and rotten plant matter. It all provided a magnificent banquet for feasting bacteria.

The cold was everywhere: in his bones, joints and flesh, inducing him to rub his neck and lower back in the hope of improving circulation to oxygenise the muscles. He recalled swallowing some of the filthy water by accident, which forced him to reflect on the consequences. What state would he be in if rescued or escaped by his own hands? Would it result in blood poisoning, typhoid, frostbite or foot rot? The despondent man did not even know what some of these diseases were, and what symptoms to look out for:

"Oh my God, it could mean being confined in hospital, to be poked and probed again."

The night sky opened up again as the last remnants of heavy sleet turned to drizzle before clearing completely to reveal the Universe, signalling no flood and no chance of escape that way. The moon proceeded to glide pass in all its glory. For the first time since his search for the new life all those years ago, he watched its passage. Even this waning celestial object was turning its back on him. Dogs were on occasions heard barking perhaps due to loneliness and the desire for company or maybe just hunger. The high pitch cry of a bird followed by the fluttering of wings suggested that it was being carried off in the mouth of some night prowler. It expressed an honest type of terror, thrashing in fear and only seconds away from death. As he contemplated death, an eerie grey haze ringed the moon. By having burnt all his bridges, there would be no lingering memories of him held by anyone. No funeral with the mourners reminiscing his life. If this pit were to be his grave then the worms would not have trouble finding him in his eternal sleep. Its previous use as a cesspit meant the place was already known as a good eatery with no disputes about paying for the bill.

Bravery or any other assigned characteristic never came into it. There was no one to observe or classify his behaviour. Recently dwelling on guilt or big questions was not normally a characteristic of his temperament. Now, these feelings came and went, as the cold dissipated them or new efforts to escape blanked his mind. What weighed the heaviest on his mind in the sobering moments was the rift with his family. The stubbled soaked man tried to recall something his father had said, almost remembered it, but it slipped to the back of his mind.

He dozed off a couple of times, only to quickly open his eyes when his body collided with the wall or when his knees buckled underneath him. His skin felt icy and turned a shade of blue. Asserted effort was required to stop his teeth from chittering, involuntarily forcing the expenditure of his dwindling energy levels. It felt like five in the morning but it could have been any time. In any case, it was unlikely that the coming of dawn with so little heat from a winter's sun would invigorate him, and its arrival would probably only signal a prolonged death; it may be kinder if another day was not seen.

The ewe did not have a good night either. It had its own small shed attached to a south-facing wall of the house but Martin's earlier shenanigans denied it any rest. The shouting, the persistent coming and goings of the intruders in need of the toilet and the never-ending irritating brightness of the house through the night then denied its normal place of sleep during the worse of the night's inclement weather. It could not seek out the highest ground to snuggle down into because the house held it. It reluctantly skulked down towards the wood to find some cover until the worse of the storm passed. This move did not bring any respite as it continued to endure a depraved night of sleep not just because of the weather but also the trepidation created by the presence of what lay in the woods. The need to stay put to keep as warm as possible and the instinct to run away from unsettling conditions battled it out in its mind. The nocturnal world had an unsettling presence on all diurnal creatures. In the end, the ewe shivered away like its master.

An hour before dawn, it went very cold, dark and extraordinarily quiet. The peering skywards prisoner remembered that a supposed sign of madness was the development of a strong fondness for seeing sunrises. Out into the silence above him as water trickled down the walls, he again screamed to dissipate his claustrophobic induced frustrations. Then in the first faint light of day, all became visible again, but only in monochrome. The absence of heat and surrounding dampness kept the air moist and worse still the stagnant water now went above the knees to thoroughly numb his legs. Rustling sounds of foraging animals and of early morning birds looking for worms could be heard above him. Scurrying rooks stared down the pit for a brief curious moment then continued presumably looking for that early worm. Later the sound of human activity reached him. The sore-headed peasants were awake, in the need of the toilet and completely unconcerned about a hard decision that lay ahead. Unease due to the ramifications of their actions had not yet gripped them. The bluster amongst them was still holding. No one was yet brave enough to express a conciliatory option for the next big decision to make.

The early morning silence and brighter sky had encouraged the ewe to return to its abode to seek its regular treat. Before heading off to work, Martin and the ewe would share breakfast in the stone floored kitchen. It ate oats while he swallowed yesterday's bread soaked in a small bowl of hot coffee mixed with instant powdered chocolate. This morning the bleary-eyed herbivore stretched its legs and trotted into the kitchen to find a dishevelled bleary-eyed carnivore fumbling the operation to make a hot drink by trying to gorge open a reluctant tin of coffee with an unsuitable heavy butcher knife.

****

Refreshed the best they could considering the night just spent but still not in a fit state to do any Sunday morning chores prior to going to mass, the intruders left the shelter of the house and gathered round the pit to again empty their bladders. First, one of them threw an empty brandy bottle on the body below; it stirred. The captive was miraculously alive, softened up, suffering from hyperthermia with a face full of bruises and scratches and bloodshot eyes but still breathing and squinting up at them.

"Have a drink while it is still warm," snorted one of them.

Then the bloodied carcass of the sheep with its throat cut and inners spawning was thrown down onto Martin. A peel of laughter was followed by final farewell insults at their captive:

"Here is your girlfriend!"

"Enjoy yourself, we did."

"I am English, not Welsh!" came the hoarse pugnacious retort.

Exhausted, beaten but still defiant, Martin chuckled when a familiar Yorkshire voice came to him:

"There's nothing so certain in life than daft folk" or was it dead folk.

A LOVE STORY

"Carry out the instructions. My counterpart at the internal affairs department has already approved authorisation for your visit. I require more than a perfunctory investigation but do not gild the lily. Your expenses will be scrutinised when you come back. Hopefully, an overnight stay will suffice."

The man receiving these instructions had nodded in a placating manner when the orders were read out to him. He doubted the cost-effectiveness of this passed down assignment. The thirty-year-old thought what was the point of being based in the most bureaucratic country in Europe and not using its numerous administrative departments to collate the desired information. At least the task would break the torpid monotony compounded by the oppressive summer afternoon heat with the build-up of stifling car fumes that polluted *Paris*.

"Have you any questions?"

"Cannot the information be requested from the local prefecture by phone or post?"

"Normally we would but this request for information has come from an unusual channel so best we appear to be more thorough with this one. I will have to vet your findings to boot, as I have not had many dealings with this lot. Remember to pick up a cell phone on the way out and do not forget your documentation or the Frenchies will just send you all the way back here to start again."

"Yes, sir."

"Remember to keep your mind on the business in hand and no digressions."

"Understood sir."

"Well, what are you waiting for?"

"I do not have any transport. I will require a car?"

"Fine, fine. I will sign off an approval to get you a pool car. No, wait. First, check the train services for that part of the world, may as well try to save money."

On the way down to his office in the basement, the man took advantage of being upstairs by having another drink from the always nearly full water cooler placed in an ostentatious hallway. A drink was required after spending around an hour in a stuffy private office with the French windows firmly closed to keep out the incessant noise of traffic jamming the streets of the administrative centre of France, the 8th arrondissement. Apart from the office furnishings and the dress sense of the occupants, everything else associated with the building was opulent Second Republic.

The youngish man was a junior diplomat based at the British consul offices on the *Rue d'Anjou,* situated on the right bank of the *Seine.* The 8th was, together with the 1st, 9th, 16th and 17th arrondissement, one of Paris's main business districts. In fact, it was the place of employment of more people than any other single arrondissement in the capital. It was also the location of many places of interest, among them the *Champs-Élysées,* the *Arc de Triomphe* and the *Place de la Concorde,* along with the *Élysée Palace,* the official residence of the President of France. Working in a district where merchants could charge whatever they liked for anything was full of daily irritations for the junior diplomat with a particular irk being the need to regularly buy bottled water. Every Monday and Wednesday, a small fortune was paid for a six-bottle pack of Jura water to sustain him downstairs at the rear of the building where the water coolers were invariably empty by the early afternoon.

Going by the size of the windows and lack of circulating air, the shared office space downstairs was probably once storage for a basement kitchen or a private cell for a resident friar. In this part of the building, there were no thick carpeted corridors with painted portraits hanging on the walls, only durable concrete floors and ceramic wall tiles that turned the narrow corridors into echo chambers, ensuring that the voices of colleagues and footsteps were a constant reminder that he was not alone. The cleanliness of the nearest toilet was not the best and reflected badly on his employers. The last time this floor was renovated was over thirty years ago. How could his employers be trusted to do anything right if the basics for human dignity could not be provided for all the staff?

It would be his first assignment outside the confines of the consulate where his time was spent saying a courteous no to non-Europeans seeking permits to live in the country of his birth. Both his parents were teachers who dedicated his childhood to get him through the education system so that their son could progress further than them. This devotion helped him get top marks at high school and then pass entrance exams at a top college at *Cambridge*. From there, the diplomatic service beckoned after he came down from *Cambridge* to seek employment. The young man amply demonstrated the qualities required by the service, a service that demanded its staff to be cold-blooded, presentable, punctilious and punctual.

It had been difficult to adjust to life in the service. There was no family background to fall on; no learning by osmosis, and being a northerner, he stood out at staff gatherings. Studying at *Cambridge* did oblige him to work on his speech; slowed it down and eliminated as much guttural utterances as possible; nonetheless, it was never going to be perfect. The top brass used his differences to illustrate to external modernisation pressure groups how it was embracing all of society, so long as the chosen candidate conformed to what was expected of him. Being a newcomer was not a new experience for him. His life had been spent breaking glass ceilings. On the plus side, he did have the natural poise for the required role and obeying orders did not bother him. Never fussed when told to drop current cases at short notice; any mistakes later found due to maladministration of uncompleted cases could be apportioned to just obeying his superior's orders. Anyway, each department had its stock of plausible excuses when performance did not meet expectations with fault effortlessly buried when human error or a cockup occurred.

His apprenticeship was served in the African continent by learning to reject every undesirable face that wanted a visa or giving a strict bureaucratic telling off to tourists who had mislaid travel documents. It was an easy apprenticeship based in a country with no historical link or influence so there were absolutely no legal or moral reasons for granting entry into England, as the rest of the world called the UK. The application rejections were handled with a stern strong refusal while maintaining sang-froid in a hot climate. If the applicant were high up in the food chain then a superior would have handled that application with kid gloves. The upshot was Mister No spent five inconspicuous years living a comfortable pressure free life, with plantation house accommodation and servants to boot. To some back home, it sounded like a good life but the reality was somewhat different. Nothing ever happened at this outpost and enriching distractions were few and far between. Any of his progeny did have the right to free education at a private school so securing the family's dream of getting on the upper echelons that produced self-perpetuating elites. However, this highly educated young man was not entirely happy with the circumstances of his part in safeguarding the genes. A dull, safe future weighed heavily on the young man. An unexciting job and a dull social life was a poor return after working so hard to reach this supposedly desirable position. His career had stalled, or probably more likely someone higher up had decided this was as far as it went. Nothing exciting lay in front of him with no possibility of extended leave to escape the monotony for a couple of years.

With applied energy, the junior diplomat persevered to obtain a position in Europe and got his move to France after several internal submissions to work in a more cultured society, same role, but a position in one of the most important European countries. On paper, the escape to the better life had been accomplished but there was the inevitable downside. He had to fend for himself in one of the most expensive and congested cities in the world. There were always small bills to be paid. Every week money was spent on getting his washing and ironing done so that every day he looked pristine despite not having a role that involved meeting anyone of importance or until this assignment working outside the consulate. Private transport was troublesome and, on his salary, unjustifiably too expensive. The need to live within his means forced him to take the *Metro* to go back and forth to an affordable arrondissement, to live on the top floor flat of a Second Republic apartment block with a kitchen the size of a cupboard and the incessant roosting noise of pigeons for company. There was no getting away from Second Republic architecture. A mock style even adorned the buildings on the circus overlooking a grand Victorian park where he was brought up.

There was not a uniform to mark him as different, but standardised formal British made dress was implied. A good clothes allowance helped and allowed prim tailored garments to be bought from government approved merchants visiting UK embassies with catalogues and samples of their wares. For casual clothes and treats like English breakfast tea and good sandwich making bread, *M&S* was available.

Social contract with the French was minimal. Like all over-crowded cities, people kept themselves to themselves. The only way for citizens to obtain solitude or privacy was by creating barriers by being rude or by the wearing of earphones to have desirable noise permanently cut out all unnecessary contact with others.

On re-entering his own office, the junior diplomat swaggered in like *James Bond* and informed his colleague that the fort had to be managed without him for a couple of days. He was off on a hush-hush mission for the old boy upstairs. The need to know gave the recipient a higher status over the uninformed. The next couple of hours were spent passing his in-tray to the downtrodden colleague with banal instructions on what tasks were more urgent. It was as if, the man had no experience of working in this department; just off the boat instead of having held this post much longer than him: held it for four years longer in fact. When it was time to leave, in mocking revenge for being left to do all the work, the young exiting diplomat was told to not forget his *Walther PKK*. It could be dangerous where he was going.

Next morning, the impromptu investigator of missing persons navigated his way across *Paris* to catch an early morning southbound *TGV*. When looking up the *SNCF* timetables the day before, he found that with one transfer he could get to his destination in fewer than three hours. On the train, his instructions were brought to mind as the train whooshed towards *Lyon*. A UK subject had disappeared and the last known whereabouts were around *Mâcon*. Reading between the lines the foreign office or security services must have requested this investigation. What interest these departments had in this region of France was neither here or there, the junior diplomat had only been sent out to find as much information as possible. After bemoaning the denial of a car, it was reflected that the cool comfort of the train was much better than a hot sticky drive in the summer heat. Before realising it, he had been deposited off at *Lyon* and forty minutes later, via a branch line, a train entered the last known whereabouts of the subject under investigation.

A taxi took him to the prefecture headquarters, a grand Second Republic limestone building. At the reception, the visitor was informed to wait and take a seat until the phone that had just rung was answered. The sitting area was under the staircase, which curved, as it swept upwards. This area had the typical glossy brochures and posters telling the good citizens how good the administration were doing at providing excellent services. Like all modern organisations, there was a need for them to create a marketing and press department to justify the reason for their existence. The answered phone calls seemed to have gone on for ages and had an element of socialising about them before the receptionist condescended to ask the visitor what was the purpose of the visit. The contact details in his official documentation were passed to the disapproving looking receptionist. Over half an hour later, an overweight middle-aged bumptious bureaucrat with ribbons on his jacket pompously arrived to tell him that his papers were in order, and a delegated assistant to help provide answers to any requests he raised would see him shortly. Making a show of it, the bureaucrat announced that his department was too busy with important affairs to allow him to spent time on this trivial matter.

After another wait, an assistant in the form of a young Algerian ethnic woman arrived and greeted him in a friendlier manner. He instinctively stood up and fleetingly narrowed his eyes and smiled at the woman. She rightly made the correct assumption that the visitor was of a rank similar to her own. It was the only way to explain why she was told to provide help for him. She was detailed the role of chaperone because of her lower position, and without hard evidence to prove it because of her gender. The pair only had enough time to sign him in, take him upstairs to an open planned office, unload his belongings then head for lunch. Walking into the office with his briefcase in one hand and an overnight bag over the other shoulder, all eyes looked up and dwelled on him for an uncomfortable few moments. He always expected this first-time reaction from others. The only surprise was his defensive reaction always annoyed him. No matter how many times he wanted to rise above the novelty of being seen as a new face, lack of confidence or more probably the absence of arrogance due to his northern upbringing stopped him from succeeding.

The newly formed team headed off to a restaurant by the quay facing the *Saône* for a leisurely two-hour lunch. Soup, lamb cutlets with a green side salad, a fruit tart followed by cheese and coffee. A jug of wine and of water helped the food go down. The junior diplomat could not help thinking that the woman was treating the lunch as a date and not as an informal meeting to ascertain the ground rules for his visit. The young woman rightly assumed the visitor was paying so was determined to enjoy lunch with a few glasses of wine.

She liked the look of the visitor. Because of her background, she found finding a good intelligent date difficult so these types of opportunities were rare for her. She casually ascertained that the man was not married and lived alone in *Paris*. She told him that she too was single and would be happy to show him around the town in the evening. When the junior diplomat ventured to mention business, he was quickly informed that administration business could not be discussed in any form outside of the prefecture headquarters; a pleased look appeared on her face when she said this impossible to disagree with declaration.

The junior diplomat grew to like her directness, very northern or in her case a very southern attitude. The thought then occurred to him that he came from the north and she the south, both born far from the administrative centres of his or her country. The thought occurred to him that for power to be effective European states required capital cities to be based within the same narrow altitude. When this idea was expressed to his guest, she replied:

"Just like the planets, too close to the sun, they get burnt out by the heat and too far out cold freezes them."

It was not exactly what was meant but her interpretation made him chuckle. She liked his happy face and told him so. To ensure the message got through to him, she left her hand gently on his when the door was held open on the way out of the restaurant. His resistance to her charms weakened further.

In the office, she started using his first name
without being invited. The woman performed her
tasks efficiently with a high level of concentration.
Electronic information and paper files on the
required individual were searched and copies
supplied to him. She translated obscure French
terminology into easily understood French and
English when possible. The man collated the
information into a format, order and language
expected from his department. He surreptitiously
glanced at the woman as she worked through the
file systems.

At the end of the day, not much illuminating
information had been gathered on the subject. It
only inferred that the subject had no money
concerns as payments had been promptly paid until
the money ran out of his bank account several years
ago. There were no concerns at all or the need for
debt collectors to attempt to track him down. No
evidence existed to suggest the use of social services.
A rebate for livestock caught his eye. When
payments from the bank stopped, the local authority
continued to send out late payment warnings until a
final note was recorded in his local tax file for
property, utilities and garbage collection. It stated
that no one at this moment lived at the property.
The file was closed under the heading of left
property abandoned without passing forwarding
address.

The young woman had phoned the individual's last
employers, *La Poste*, and found out that the subject
had worked for them for three years then one

February did not turn up. No notice was given. The man had just stopped working. After a warning letter was sent, the employee was formally given his sacking orders in writing. No one went round to his house. The personnel file on him had few details, and none that gave clues about his nature: no warnings or praise had been recorded.

"Immigrant workers come or go all the time. The management would not have been too concerned," volunteered his helper.

"Would the postman not notice anything?"

"It is hard to say as the post may not be delivered to the subject's door but left at a pickup point near it."

The young woman arranged appointments for the next day with the *agents immobilier* that sold the property to the subject and the police. A late start was planned to allow him to rest after his travels. On the way out of the prefecture building, she escorted him to the hotel that was booked for him. She insisted that it was no problem and wanted to make sure the stranger to her town was settled, and she would know where to come later in the evening to accompany him to dinner: it was her duty to entertain the visitor and allow him to appreciate the delights of *Mâcon*.

"Best to eat with someone than alone," she insisted.

When she left him in the hotel her scent lingered like the thrill of her accidental hand touch at the restaurant.

It had been a long day so the junior diplomat happily collapsed on the bed for a forty-minute nap before showering the sweat off him. Sleep failed to arrive as the thought of vanishing without a trace dwelled on his mind; not the disappearance of the subject but of himself. His past was contemplated, a habit that had recently manifested itself when feelings of ennui and unrest raised doubts. It had been fine for a while but there must be more to life than this. Shared leisure activities were invariably sport of some type, like cricket with the Aussie delegation or baseball with the big cousin. The recent declaration of war against terror by the Leader of the Free World after the Twin Towers Attack had curtailed many of these activities. One could say he had been denied admission into the real world; never to be happy or even content, had become an exile in a big city, living a zombie-like existence.

Just turned thirty, another twenty-five years of this humdrum routine lay ahead of him.

To lessen the tedium, some staff escaped into a fantasy world. With regards to the old office colleague, it was a case of hiding by reading and re-reading *sci-fi* novels and probably comics, imagining himself in a world of talking robots, aliens and nanobots maintaining his fragile body or turning it into one of superhuman strength, probably dreaming about a sexless and even humanless future. Suffice to say, this man must have loved this posting for the high profile that *la bande dessinée* had in France. However, when talking it was clear that he no longer differentiated between fact and fiction; all the while conveying an inane affliction of possessing narrow tastes and mores of a bye-gone age; and having the annoying habit whenever in company to continually check his watch, creating the acute impression that life was a great inconvenience to him. The young diplomat never understood how this person reconciled the seemingly juxtapose positions of his professed belief in a God with a life spent reading fiction. A dilettante entrenched in *sci-fi,* hiding from the fantastic truth about the creation of the Universe. Did this man ever consider what would happen on *Judgement Day* when asked how he had used the gift of life?

In some ways, it would have been advantageous for the young diplomat if Man had already created nanobots to continually circulate in the human body. The elimination of the perpetual cold that this colleague endured, or more appropriately, others had to suffer would have been most welcomed. No coaxing could persuade this natural stony bachelor to seek medical help, a stubborn man who probably never in his life worried about his appearance or understood why people copulated. Completely unconcerned about nasal hair protracting out of his nose, on the hour, every hour, a handkerchief would be removed from his trouser pocket to loudly blow his nose to pedantically see what his sinuses had to offer.

Others, according to the recent warnings on personal behaviour, appeared to be sexual deviants or alcoholics putting the nation's secrets at risk. The higher echelons fretted about the impact on the standing of the service if the press founded out that junior staff spent all their free time either pissed out of their heads, consorting with prostitutes in *Pigalle* or worse still, dressed in women's clothing or squeezed into living doll latex. As for him, every night was spent in his flat without the consolation of drink or drugs to help him sleep, while neighbours all around him were noisily banging away.

A sudden arousal forced him out of bed and into the shower room where the gushing water restored his composure. He then meticulously dressed for dinner.

At his suggestion, the pair ate in the hotel as it would keep the receipts simpler and conceal the fact that he had entertained. It was a similar meal to that enjoyed at lunchtime except for the choice of vegetables was much better and the meat slower cooked. The wine was more expensive to boot. She found his mannerism amusing and strangely quaint. Afterwards, the young couple strolled out into the night air to walk along the quay festoon with coloured festive bulbs of red and yellow discretely suspended above the water edge: a romantic walk for lovers to watch the glimmer of the moon off the waters and the sparkle of the stars. They ended up at *Chez Pierre*, her choice. From the outside, the atmosphere appeared jolly as customers mingled together in a bright interior full of alcoholic paraphernalia on the walls. Some tables were placed outside on the quieter street for couples that desired a more intimate chat.

Once served at the bar, they stood like everyone else to soak up the atmosphere. The normal table service was pointless if customers preferred to stand. After about fifteen minutes, they sat outside as the young woman was having difficulty in understanding his French against the background chatter. They quickly got accustomed to the once-overs from passing promenaders and oblivious to the happy murmur of the drinkers in the bar behind them. Everything was peaceful as cool air came in from the river. As far as he could observe the Algerian was not that different from many of the other women that passed by. Same, wonderful tanned Mediterranean skin, shiny black hair and dark eyes radiating confidence. Her natural scent was of olives and heat infused herbs. Any differences were slight and only ascertained by the sharp-eyed.

Time drifted away as the two of them silently remained seated with the same pulse beating, enjoying the night with two empty glasses on the table that a waiter never came to take away. They sat until one in the morning observing the strolling world of youth.

Later, lying in bed, he observed how funny that you could clearly see the outline of a woman's body when she was a stranger but when in close contact the outline became blurred by her personality. His deprived senses were shaken and stirred.

In the morning, the investigators strolled round to the *agents immobilier*, and met the same person that sold the property all those years ago. The

English buyer had seen the house and location and immediately wanted it. Other than remembering raising a surprise when the property was bought with a cheque from a German bank, nothing unusual was recalled. The professional salesman then described in flowing tones the house and natural aspects to be viewed from it. After this sales pitch, the pair sought refreshments at a delicatessen. A coffee with a pastry allowed them to eat up time until the next appointment at the police station.

This appointment was also fruitless. Nothing was gathered to suggest anything out of place. No one reported him missing. A check of his bank account had shown no suspicious withdrawals. The *canton* was known to be quiet with a self-policing population; no one could remember the last time a serious crime had been reported; it was unheard of.

The woman suggested that a car be hired to drive out to the deserted house.

"We can have lunch on the way there," added as an incentive.

Before leaving the consulate, the hiring of a car once arrived in *Mâcon* had not been broached. However, it was the logical thing to do, so he agreed.

Waiting for cool air to circulate through the opened doors of a sunshine yellow *Peugeot 206*, the woman slipped off her jacket and silk scarf while the man removed his jacket and tie. She revealed a collarless

V-neck rose coloured silk blouse and he a lightly coloured sky blue short-sleeve oxford shirt. Once in the passenger seat, she checked her makeup by pouting her lips at the rear-view mirror, brushed her hair, got her sunglasses out of her handbag and sunk back to enjoy the view. When the junior diplomat asked her what road to take, she admitted to rarely venturing out of town and only knew roughly where the farmhouse was located. However, she told him there was no need to worry, as better directions will be obtained from the patron of the roadside restaurant they would stop at. Before turning the ignition, the man attempted to find out the exact location for himself by punching the road name given by the *notaire* into the provided *Sat Nav*. The refreshed display just suggested the direction of travel with no precision on the location of the farmhouse; technological advancement for such detail was still to catch up on this good idea for an aid to car travel.

As the car drove out of town, the young woman appeared to become sullen. She chatted about how immigrants and their descendants felt uneasy when in the countryside of the adopted country. It seemed that artificial forces allowed all races to co-exist in cities but an instinctive prohibition prevailed in the countryside, an invisible barrier that prevented the spread of multiculturalism. Out of kindness, the young diplomat suggested that she should apply reverse psychology by thinking that the problem lay with the indigenous people who retreated to the fringes when a stronger culture entered the towns and cities. In any case, he reminded her that non-

European migrants concentrated their efforts to become independent shop owners and entrepreneurs, not farmers; they wanted freedom from slavery to the land.

Brightening up, she casually asked him if he had read any French literature. He said he had read some. This encouraged her to voice her opinion:

"Great writers know how to create good social dialogue. They are all playwrights at heart."

She then coquettishly expressed an observation in the hope of stirring a reaction from the driver:

"You are not great at expressing feelings. Are you shy?"

Above the heat from the engine and sun, the driver detected his cheeks warming.

Lunch was basic and served its purpose with the added bonus of the patron pointing out on the provided hired car roadmap where precisely was the district and the minor road they wanted to travel on. A good result for him and her, as she gathered more information about her new friend. The earlier nudge to open him up had worked.

The first impressions of the found farmhouse did match the claims of the *notaire*. The hill position and the views across the valley were picturesque. The young woman indicated with a pointing arm the direction where the grapes grew for *Beaujolais* wine. It was also a peaceful place. In the bright sunlight, the only sounds to be heard were that of buzzing flies and bees and the high pitch cry of a watchful bird. It was easy to forget that there was work to be done. Regaining a business-like persona, the pair marched into the vacated house, hesitated as some startled birds flapped into the air and flew out of the broken windows. It was apparent that no one had lived here for years. The interior was a mess, the weather, animals and birds had dilapidated the place. What remained of the window blinds fluttered in the breeze. Nothing was clean and any breakable was broken. Insects had created a world where they persistently fought to create or defend empires to allow them the right to consume all other organic materials.

Checking the *Blackberry*, a text message instructed him to phone the consulate. His superior was probably getting impatient for feedback and worried about his spending. Returning the call, he was surprised by the excellent signal strength and reflected that European countries that were inward thinking and had given up on demanding a powerful world presence had better infrastructure. The phone conversation was initially terse on his part: abandoned house, been missing for a long time, no official records to suggest anything about the subject, except that money was not an issue, it came from Germany, and officialdom only took an interest when bills remained unpaid after his bank account stop paying out. Without hard facts and the need to say something more his imagination then ran ahead of him:

"Could he have been an informer given a new identity that was not good enough to hide him?"

The superior abruptly interrupted him to remind him that his role was to provide facts, not suppositions. If there was nothing to give an indication of why the subject went missing, leave it at that and return to *Paris*. Placing the cell phone in his pocket, he noticed the woman staring at him with a look that had a hint pleading behind it as she bit her lip. After a few moments of thought, the young diplomat suggested that a drive about the *canton* would give him a better feel of the place.

"What is down the other side of the road?"

"Probably old France, a close-knit community clinging to the land for millennia."

"Nothing wrong with a close-knit community."

"City folk pay for their existence?"

"Your agricultural policy does infuriate the politicians in my country. Nonetheless, there are costs to bear by rounding them up and herding them into large housing settlements to fester and rot away."

It only took a few minutes to reach the hamlet at the bottom of the hill. It was now late afternoon and the place was quiet, waiting for the workers to come home from the fields to get washed and fed. The car stopped near a shop, when exited, as usual, the young diplomat immediately became aware of the sensation of being watched, in this case, it was realised that the uncomfortable feeling was probably due to the depiction of the agony of *Christ* looking down on him. The young woman wanted a packet of *blondes* and stated that they could always ask at the counter about the foreigner up the hill. He agreed while thinking about why young French women smoke so much. Several minutes passed at a deserted counter before a door at the rear opened to allow an ancient looking woman to come out of the shadows. It was the same server as on that night, a bit more diminutive, more ashen looking with leaden watery eyes, but just as unforgivingly obstinate. Her eyes stared out of a scrawny creased face, for all of the world, it looked like a shawl adorned grey heron was dressed by eager kids running amok with everything they could lay their hands on. When asked by the young woman if she knew what had happened to the house up the road, the disinterested server caustically replied:

"No, nothing."

Holding out her hand, she demanded payment for the cigarettes:

"Money, money."

The young diplomat intervened and asked if the old woman remembered the foreign postman.

"No, money."

Outside the shop, the young diplomat commented that the old woman did not take a liking to his chaperone. She replied that the intransient soul was not keen on him either. The smiling snubbed pair strolled to the car and decided to continue the drive around the area. Perspiration formed on their arms and foreheads as imperceptible facial movements hinted at the fruitlessness of this arbitrary slow run to get a feel for the *canton*. Looking out onto the pastures, the woman expressed her sympathy at what was observed:

"Peasants spend their whole lives digging."

Changing the subject, the deep in thought driver aired the view that the missing man must have been good at his job to remember all the tucked away homesteads round here.

The untrained investigator decided that they were getting nowhere and seeing nothing that was not a picture postcard of yesteryears. He was flummoxed and felt far out of his depth. There were no answered questions because they found out nothing about the subject's life here nor had they discovered any facts about his disappearance. Nothing had been found out about the man, why he stayed here, what had happened to him and where he was now. Even cold case detectives would struggle. Reading his thoughts, the young woman sighed in his right ear:

"There are lots of places around here that could hide a body with no chance of accidental discovery."

The young diplomat decided to have one more look

at the derelict farmhouse, to make a more careful survey of the premises:

"Maybe, a hint somewhere will reveal the whereabouts or the reason for the disappearance of the subject."

He switched on the *Sat Nav* to just see how it would perform down in the valleys, again the precision was poor but knowing the direction of travel helped, so after one wrong turn, the car re-entered the hamlet and sped up the hill.

At the permanently opened entrance gate, the young diplomat stopped the car and checked the mailbox, nothing; it looked as if it had been used as a nest by a lateral thinking bird. They then drove along the gravel path overwhelmed by grass and weeds, stopped again and got out. He invited the woman to smoke one of her purchased cigarettes as he took another look round the house. Before reaching the front door, he turned round and called out:

"He must have had transport?"

The young woman nodded.

Although the same birds as earlier repeated a similar panicking escape when he entered the house, the character of the interior was different. The blinds were no longer swaying. The lower rays of light had fashioned darker shadows in the impenetrable parts of each entered room while other parts appeared to be flooded by strong light. Taking his time, he sifted through the filth and wreckage, picking up and discarding articles as he went along. Amid the mess, the young diplomat wondered what happened here. Everything that a man living alone required was still here, but there was nothing personal to indicate a past life. Upstairs, even the bathroom portrayed a manly existence with a toothbrush, safety razor and some rusty blades left on a grime-encrusted shelf. The occupant must have lived a simple uncomplicated life.

Finally, something drew his full attention, something that was personal. A reflected shard of light from a previously unseen half hidden small box caught his eye. It was among clothes that had been thrown onto the floor of what was once the occupied bedroom. Opening it, revealed war medals, British war medals. Tactfully closing the box, the thought occurred to him what use was a report that did not convey gathered feelings and impressions. He recalled what his superior had really wanted him to do: go through the motions and do not attempt any in-depth investigation. The fact was if a proper investigation were the intention then the consulate would not have sent a junior diplomat. With the box in his hand, the young man slowly descended the stairs taking care not to put his foot through any woodworm rotted step and met up with the woman again. She was round the back, near a cluster of forget-me-nots, staring at the wild meadow around her, full of summer colour created without any help from Man. Before them, poppies, thistles, ragwort, hogweed, bindweed and knapweed along with daisies and buttercups all competed for the attention of the pollinators. Both silently thought it would be a nice place to raise a family.

"What will happen to this place?"

"If it remains abandoned for much longer, the state will repossess it and sell it on," replied the young woman.

"The location is good. Someone could turn the place around. Modernise it. Maybe, add a wind turbine and solar panels to it."

"Yes, the vineyards have already started to exploit free energy."

The young man looked across at the house and dwelled on the possibility of knocking it down and replacing it with a modern functional structure ideal for contemporary living. Sustainability with comfort and easy maintenance by using technological innovation to get want you wanted with reduced expenditure on utility bills. Build something with style and colour, more panache; the sort of family home seen in the colour supplements of Sunday papers.

"A rowan tree would look nice here. You can tell by the growth that the soil is good here."

"Why a rowan tree," asked the woman.

"It is something northerners in my country do to bring luck to a house."

"Silly northerners," laughed the pleased woman.

"Yes."

The woman then noticed the horseshoe above the front door:

"If you believe in luck then that horseshoe has to be turned the other way round, as at the moment it is set to give bad luck."

Realising that the man was confused, she explained in France good luck was given when the ends of the shoe pointed down.

A moment later, the young diplomat again allowed his mind to wander.

"Did he have the bottle to pack it all in, to search for a better life.

He would definitely stand out here.

What sort of children would an Algerian and him produce?

What would his parents, or her parents for that matter think?

What a surprise for the local school if their kids turned up.

Would it be too silly to try?

His old granny would flip her lid. She wanted him to marry one of the granddaughters of her siblings still living in the old country.

Maybe she would come around to the idea knowing that the woman was born of the Faith."

The couple stood side-by-side, hands almost touching, observing the sun briefly disappear behind a lone cloud. A tall elegant Pakistani ethnic man alongside a modern thinking twenty-something French born Algerian; both with excellent symmetrical profiles, intelligent eyes and a need for an understanding companion.

Without any further procrastination, he decided to stay on longer, take the wrath of his superior, and the next day go around to the post sorting office, to try and discover personal and social details of the presumed lost man by asking the right people: personnel that worked every day with this man and would have observed his movements. His accommodating aide would resume the search of official documentation to determine how the man travelled about.

Their time together could not end right this. The unexplained had to be explainable.

"When we remember we are all mad, the
mysteries disappear and life stands explained,
Mark Twain."